Apple Tree

a novel

by

Katharina Schlager

For Christian

PROLOGUE: A GREAT STORY

"There once was a great writer. He had been searching for an important story. For his story. The great one any writer hopes to write one day. Even though he didn't tell anyone about it, he was getting more and more pressured. He sat down every day to write. Every day he put down words after words. Every night he went to bed a little more disheartened. A little more defeated. A little more resentful. A little more afraid. The more he searched, the more he started to be bored with the ideas he came up with. Ashamed even. They seemed to be so irrelevant. So benign. So lame. So inconsequential.

He told his publisher, that he was working on something great. They believed him. He had never disappointed. He was a great writer after all. But it had been a while since he had delivered something publishable. Years. Nevertheless, they believed him. Why wouldn't they? That made him even more nervous and despairing in his search. He did not want to disappoint their expectations. Destroy his self-image. Lose his idea of self-worth.

So he kept searching and searching. Until... well... writer's block hit him hard. He sat at his desk. And he stared. The words just would not come. Not even the irrelevant ones. The benign. The lame. The inconsequential.

He could not see the fruit in his garden. Ripe to be harvested.

He stopped eating healthily. He stopped talking to his neighbours. He stopped calling his daughter and refused to pick up the phone. They might all see through him. The fraud. The great writer. Great writer, my arse, he thought and poured himself another cup of thick black coffee.

The apple tree in his now overgrown garden had one particularly thick sturdy branch. High up that one was. He had been thinking a lot about that thick sturdy rope in the attic, they had used to tow his car once. The one he had bought for his daughter's tree house, when she was little. The one in the apple tree. If he wanted to do something about his situation, he did not want to go to any shop to get equipment beforehand. He needed to do this here. On his own. On his own terms. Witnessed by none. It would be really horrible, if he had to go to the shops to buy a rope. He would anticipate questions about what he wanted it for. Though probably no-one would care. But would that not be worse? He did not want to go to all the different chemists in town to stack up on sleeping pills either. Buy some fertilizer at the garden centre. No... whatever was already at the house would have to do.

The thick sturdy branch seemed to be able to hold his weight. It had once been home to the now long-gone tree house. It looked so inviting.

So, he went up to the attic to search for the rope instead of a story for a change. When he found it, he started to have doubts. It felt quite brittle. It had been up there in the dusty attic for over two decades now, he estimated. It would have to do, though.

It was already too late in the afternoon. Too late to tie the rope to the branch. Too late to figure out, how to make a noose. To prepare anything. As he wanted to step onto the stool, he had also found in the attic, and which would be perfect for this sad job, he would not want to second guess how the rope was tied to the branch and have more than one go at the endeavour. He would measure everything the next day and then do it as soon as the sun was down. No-one should have to see this. He did not want to see anything either. Hopefully, that was his reasoning, darkness would ease the step over to whatever came next. Or not.

He was never sure what to believe in. Or what to hope for. Would it be comfort or torture, that there was just another life waiting for him? Never being able to escape yourself for all eternity. Was an afterlife not the real hell – even in a supposed heaven? If it meant continuing with your own stupid incompetent self what was the point at all of the apple tree? If afterlife meant a relief from this torture as well... well, he might embrace it, he figured. Whatever would come next – or not... There was nothing he could do about it now or then anyway. So let's just see and find out. These thoughts made him nervous about the tree. Going into the unknown is always unsettling.

He put the rope into the big chest in the living room, where he kept all kinds of knick-knacks that still hadn't quite found a place in the house. Even though he hadn't had any visitors for a long time, he did not want to take any chances of anyone seeing the rope in the open. All those possible questions.

He would tie it to the apple tree as late in the afternoon as possible for the same reason. The bushes and trees around the edges of his property had grown so high by now, none of neighbours had taken a peak into his outdoor life for a long time. Still... you couldn't be too careful.

The apple tree stood in a spot that was hard to see from any gap that might exist in the vegetal wall around his life.

The rope in the chest, the plan set in his head, he poured himself another coffee and sat down on the patio. Then something strange and unexpected happened. For the first time in months he was able to hear the birds singing. He was able to see the beautiful butterflies flapping their wings. Smell the flowers, growing unchecked and lusciously. Feel the slight breeze and the warm late spring sun on his skin. He was able to breathe. Breathe.

He sat there for quite a long while. Just breathing, sipping coffee, leaning back. Not thinking about all the words out there, that might be able to form a great story. His great story. They were out there. For sure. He just wasn't able to summon them.

Find them. Put them together. But for the first time in his life, he did not care. He would let them be. Leave them out there for someone else to find. "Fuck off", he thought, smiled and sighed.

He found some pickled vegetables in his larder, some potatoes – and there was even some cream and some cheese in his fridge that had not gone off yet. He was hungry, when the sun finally went down. He was happy to find all that food, to make a decent and quite tasty meal.

That night he went to bed happy. He fell asleep quickly. But at three o'clock he woke with a start. He always kept a little notepad and pens by the side of the bed. Just in case. Though he had never used them before. In a strange half-asleep, half-awake state he started to scribble in the dark. He hadn't dreamed in months. At least not that he could remember. And when he could, it had been either very strange anxiety dreams or boring nightmares. But this night was different. He was flowing through the most lavish dreamscape. The most wonderful storyline. He had found his great story. Not only that. He knew, he had found a great truth. He had found the greatest story ever told.

He fell back on his pillow and returned to a happy relaxed dream about talking sheep and a cigar smoking dog that got swept up in a sparkly whirlwind and some other inconsequential nonsense only a very relaxed brain with no real worries could cook up.

When he woke the next morning, he immediately fumbled for his notepad and started to laugh. Of course. I am such a fool, he thought. Of course.

He jumped out of bed and got dressed in his favourite most comfortable clothes. After a trip to the supermarket, where he stocked up on wonderful food and some of his favourite wine, after he had smiled at everyone he had met on the way, wishing them a wonderful good morning, for that was indeed what it was, after all of this, he poured himself a wonderfully foaming cup of milky coffee and went to his study. He looked out of the window and laughed. Then he started to write. Full of joy.

Remembering what made him write in the first place. Oh, the excitement. His fingers could hardly follow the stream of words pouring out of him. His brain, his heart... wherever these words came from. They came so willingly. So forcefully, he was hardly able to contain the flow and pay enough attention to every word. Not missing a beat of this joyous stream.

The apple tree was hit by lightning only a few days later, breaking off the thick sturdy branch. Damaging the tree so much, it never produced any apples ever again. It was just as well. He didn't even notice. Nor did he notice the sapling that pushed its way up from a pip of an abandoned apple that had rotted and sunk into the rich soil. Unchecked, the little tree grew and fought its way towards the sun. Only after the old tree was cut down, a few years later, a few feet apart from its parent tree, the young one stretched its branches, started to blossom and eventually produced beautiful sweet red apples.

His publisher fell in love with the new book of the great writer. The readers and critics celebrated him for decades to come. He found his way back into other people's lives and started to call his daughter at least every week for a chat. He even attended all of his grandson's birthdays, bringing the best presents the boy could have ever wished for in his most secret dreams.

When the great writer died, he had a smile on his face and the congregation celebrated his friendly nature and his celebration of life itself.

On his night-stand his daughter found the notepad containing only three words: *Boy meets girl.*

It was the greatest story ever told."

TUESDAY

Triumphantly I look over to Ben. He bursts out laughing. Belly-laughs. I have never heard him laugh this hard before. I start giggling.

"What a build-up", he gasps and wipes some tears from his face.

"You looked the whole time, as if you where waiting for a punchline."

"Well...", he tries to stop laughing long enough to say something, but he is struggling. "You started out as if you were telling some joke..." (he has to pause and take a deep breath) ... "you looked like a proud teenager, who wanted to tell a dirty joke to a friend... something they had heard or read somewhere... but then you kept going and going and I had no idea, where you were going and why you were telling me this..."

He pulls the package in his arms closer to himself. Lovingly. He nods. He is still laughing. He sighs. Then he is back to staring out of the car window, watching the landscape fly by. All those fields with newly forming crops. The hopeful new start. The promise of a big harvest. Plants reaching up to get as much sun and water as they possibly can.

The package in his arms contains my story. Boy meets girl. Greatest story ever told? Perhaps not quite. I wouldn't be audacious enough to make that claim. But it is my story. And it is finished. I never thought I would get here. To this point. Sitting in the car with Ben. Holding that book. A whole book. Sure, I have still all my doubts and insecurities about my work, but I have to admit, I am impressed with myself. There it is.

Ben says that he never had any doubts of me getting here. Despite our rocky journey. All our new starts and dead ends. But then again, that is his function after all. Why would he doubt?

He keeps chuckling to himself.

"It seems you are ready to start looking for your next story", he says.

I hadn't thought about that yet. But I immediately know that he is right. There is more than that package still in there. Somewhere. So many people waiting to be brought to life. Sent on wonderful or excruciating journeys. Pain, joy, laughter, love, death... all of that still waiting somewhere to find its story.

"Possibly", is all that I can say. But I can't help beaming. I know Ben catches it. But I don't allow myself to ruin the moment by embarrassment or any other silly emotion that might belittle the exciting exhilarating prospect of writing again.

"I am glad, you threw it away ... you know... and rewrote..." Ben is stroking the package again.

"I know."

I know. I know, he is glad. It is a perfectly lovely story now. A really good one. Possibly even a little great. But not quite as genuine as the one that got me there. Still. Ben is glad. And I am glad because of that. The package is a little too cleaned up. But I got it out. This is what counts. It is a start.

We have been on the road only for a couple of hours now. Only just started this journey. We have six days till Monday. The big meeting. The moment of truth. No, that is too dramatic. The editor at the publishing house has already decided that she likes my writing. They have already decided to publish. We just need to talk details. Polish a little, maybe. Edit out spelling mistakes. The tedious fine-tuning after the frenzy of creation.

We have agreed to work through every page together. I have rented a place in the city quite close to the publisher's office. Three weeks should be plenty, she had said. Plenty. There is not much fine-tuning to do, she had cooed. We will see.

I have never done this. I don't know quite what to expect. Will she improve my story? Leave my work intact? Turn it into something completely different? Will I be able to accept changes if they make it better? Will I be able to defend my work, if she distorts it?.. I am not sure. This work that has gone through so many changes, new starts, rewrites. So many stories. So many stories before reaching this one. So much doubt and pain. So much joy as well. Ben will be by my side, I hope. He usually is nowadays. Rachel might be, too, if I am unlucky. I will have to handle her, if she is.

I could have taken a flight. I could have made this really simple. I did not want to.

A road trip. Six days, six nights. Rent a car. Cheapest model I could find. And just drive to the city. Make lots of stops on the way. Visit places. Take detours. The scenic route. I don't know. It feels as silly as it feels right.

Ben is stroking the package. The pile of pages. Those pages filled with my story. I still can't believe it is there. So neatly wrapped up in brown paper. A string to keep the paper in place. I couldn't find any sticky tape to tie it up. So the string had to do. It seems more appropriate somehow. Not quite as constricting as sticky tape would have been. But also not quite as protective, I suppose.

The landscape is changing to a small wood, when Ben finally turns back to me.

"We will have to start thinking about accommodation for tonight."

"Already ahead of you. There is a Best Western in a small town about half an hour from here. Well, roughly... I thought, I could make my first stop there. I have made a reservation."

Ben nods. I had half expected him to protest. A Best Western. A hotel chain. Not exactly trying out anything new and unexpected. He will have to give me some time to adjust. This has been quite a journey for me. I am not there yet. It is a wonder in itself, that I got here, when I think about how I started. And how I first thought it ended. All those changes. About the moment I opened that laptop and put my fingers on those unwilling keys. A small miracle. Not what I thought it would be. Not exactly the greatest story ever told. But a small miracle.

ANNA

I stare at the blinking cursor on my screen. The ideas just won't come. My fingers rest nervously on the keys of my laptop. I want to type. But there is just no sense to be made of all the letters available. The empty page. The nightmare of any writer. A writer... What a joke. I almost start laughing out of spite. Whoever put that idea in my head I could write anything. Oh Anna, you idiot. You arrogant idiot. I say this out loud and I shake my head.

I always fancied myself a writer. Early on as a child, the moment I could put words together, I wanted to write. Anything. Everything. I was sure the stories would come to me. Genius. Inspired. So easy, when you are talented. Oh Anna, you are such a talent. Oh fuck off! The empty page says otherwise. And excuses have gone. I made excuses for so long. As a journalist you write all day. Literature in a hurry. Literature for wrapping chips the next day. Or fish. That was what our editor always said, when we worried too much about already published errors. Misspelt names. Controversial opinions. Wrong dates or locations. Never mind. Yesterday's news, tomorrow's fish wraps. Local news are too quick to stick.

But when you write all day, there is no urge to write when you are not in the office. No time. No time. Excuses, excuses. All written out.

I have time now. And nothing else to write.

The first pension payment arrived in my account this morning. Very clearly it sat there on the bank statement. It had felt like being on holiday so far. Or being off sick for a bit. Or maybe in-between jobs. Very unreal. Retirement was something I had longed for. Now that it is here, it doesn't feel real. And yet, there it was. The money on the statement. The numbers. Black ink on blue paper. And then it hit me. Right there in the room with the ATMs. I have got time on my hands now. I can finally do what I want. Everything I always wanted to do. I can write. I got so excited that I almost ran home. Despite my swollen knee, that creaks every time I need to bend it. I nearly forgot to go to the shops to get some groceries. Milk. Coffee. Bread. Apples. Butter. Some vegetables. Rice. Pasta. Stuff. And lots of cheese. At home I threw the groceries in the kitchen. I had to make a real effort to put them in the cupboard or the fridge. I had forgotten ketchup. I am still annoyed about that. Not enough though to get out of the house again and make my way back to the shop. I will have to eat my dinner without it tonight.

Bloody cursor. Does it have to blink like that? Reminding me, that I am not typing right now. Come on! It says. Come on! Do it! Do it!

I need to pee. Good excuse, I guess. For now. For a few minutes. But I want to start writing. So I ignore the urge till it goes away. One sentence. Come on! Come on, bitch!... Nothing. Blank bloody page.

I have always been able to handle the first sentence of an article quite well. It comes to me quite easily. Nothing I ever had to worry about. But then again... journalism is a craft, not an art form. If you are well trained the first sentence comes to you. Not always equally easily. But it will come. The story, your subject dictates it. The facts, the quotes. It is all there before you type. You just have to shape it into something readable. Easy-peasy.

That is the problem. I don't have a story. A subject. I don't have an editor, who sends me to a car crash site, a celebration at a day care centre for the elderly because they finished building the super-modern new wing. There is no interview over the phone with the mayor about the water pipes that keep bursting in the main street on a regular basis. It is just me, my blank page and the cursor – waiting for the letters to come. Anything goes.

Fuck.

They don't come.

I close my eyes and take my hands off the keys. Coffee. Maybe that will help. Coffee usually does. At least it gives me an excuse to get up and stop staring. I have to pee first though. Desperately by now. On my way to the bathroom I take a little detour through the kitchen to switch on the coffee-maker. Let it warm up. Then I rush to the bathroom as the pressure on my bladder is starting to get borderline unbearable. It is a warm day so I am wearing a loose tank top and jeans. Maybe not the most flattering attire. I shouldn't have taken a look in the mirror though. My wobbly bits, the upper arms, the gut, are all too visible for comfort.

„Fuck off, Anna Bennik, you ugly slob.“

I flip myself the bird, pull an ugly face and then flush the toilet, before I walk back into the kitchen grumbling and cursing at myself.

I need to warm some milk and foam it. I love those moments though they are so tedious. The making of a perfect cup of coffee. Well – I say coffee... it is more a lot of milk with a bit of coffee. But that coffee needs to be right. Too strong, too bitter and I get a headache. The milk the perfect temperature.

I waddle back to my desk next to the big window with the foamy hot drink in my hand... I give myself a few moments enjoying the smell. Looking out of the window over the field, behind which the horses of the riding school are enjoying the warm sun and the lush grass on the meadow.

There is a little brook running along the path next to the field. It is perfect for long strolls. And apart from a few dog-owners you hardly ever meet anyone there. Ever. The people from the neighbourhood are all young. Very few pensioners. All working. Full-time. Successful. Lots of children. They are all in the city for their jobs, for school, for day-care. The streets are empty during the day. During the week. Even on the weekends a lot of people seem to want to get away. Take trips. I never understood why you build these beautiful houses and have these big gardens if the only ones who seem to enjoy them are the gardeners you employ. The help. The cleaners. I never employed anyone for my place. It shows. The dust bunnies have become a big feature in my home. Stains. Chaos. Worn clothes. Unfolded laundry. Dirty dishes. The garden is so overgrown that I don't dare to rip anything out, cut anything back as it will disturb its natural balance. My excuses for not handling my home are gone though. I have to get to work some time soon and sort it out a bit.

I breathe in the lovely scent of my coffee again. I take a sip and then put the cup next to the laptop. Once again I place my fingertips on the keys. Ready to type. Nothing. Just the blinking fucking cursor.

ANNA

Today is the day. I will write. I know it. I have been up most of the night, writing up a schedule. I am good at schedules. Better at writing, than keeping them, mind you. But... it is a start. I have always tried to draw up schedules throughout my professional life. Keep the chaos in my life at bay. I just lose sight of appointments and stuff. Get lost in the everyday chores and then get nothing done. To-do-lists. Big fan. So I drew up a schedule last night. Structured my weeks. I will have to keep getting up at 8 a.m., I decided. If I sleep too much I get headaches. I need a fixed point to start the day.

Already messed that up for today. It is 10.25 a.m. already and I haven't changed out of my pyjamas yet. Oh well, I will start late today. I pull a face. "Well, shut up. It was late last night", I grumble and stick my tongue out at my reflection in the kitchen window.

Right, schedule.

So, get up at 8 a.m.. Bathroom time. Sometimes shower, always brush teeth and hair, get dressed. Put in contacts and a tiny bit of foundation on. Deodorant. Done. Kitchen. Breakfast. 9 a.m. at the very latest. Coffee making celebration and thus first reason to be alive in the day. Then I go upstairs to my desk. Write till 11 a.m.. Break. Prepare lunch. Eat. Then do household chores, one hour. Depending on the day of the week that will be laundry (twice a week), cleaning the bathroom or the kitchen, hoovering, take out the trash, dusting, working in the garden, or doing anything that needs doing. After that I take a walk for an hour that might end with getting some groceries on the way back.

That should have me back in the house by 3 or 4 p.m. at the latest. Coffee and back to the desk till 8 p.m. at least. Then dinner and relax time. That should give me about six hours of writing, plus time to sort out my place and get some fresh air. Sounds like a solid plan, I guess.

I have my muesli standing next to the sink. The shop has changed brands. I hate this sugary new stuff. It will give me cramps. I can feel them coming just by tasting this sickly sweet mixture. I really should read the list of ingredients. It is so late, that I decide to skip lunch and have a meal in the evening. I pour the left-overs from my bowl into the sink, spitting out some oatmeal flakes. Go to the shops, get a different kind of cereal and a sandwich to eat on my walk.

I sigh, rub my temples. "Come on, you lazy cow." I start wobbling to the bathroom scratching my bum. Half an hour later I look presentable and walk out of the front door.

10 p.m. I have written something. Half a page. Real drivel. My mind keeps slipping. I feel like there is someone in the house with me. This is rubbish of course. I also don't know why I would think that. I haven't seen or heard anyone. There are no creaking floor boards. No weird shadows. Just a feeling in my stomach. What is surprising to me, I don't feel scared. No irrational panic attack or fantasy of an axe-wielding maniac, wandering through my house. Just a knowledge that I am not alone. I should go to bed now. Otherwise I won't be able to keep the schedule.

I delete all the words again and slam my laptop shut.

ANNA

He is beautiful, with his wavy auburn hair. The fine outline of his face. The thin nose. The high cheekbones. Those small blue eyes. Soulful. Amused. He is sitting in the big armchair on the opposite side of the room to my desk. He has been waiting there for me, when I come up the stairs with my steaming hot coffee. So handsome. Kind. He must be tall. It is hard to tell. He is sitting after all.

I know a lot of children have imaginary friends. Older brothers, that has never been born. Friends to pass the time with. Or make up for the lack of real ones. I never had one as a child. I didn't expect him to be so vivid. My imagination was always a little too rational, cynical even, for such a fanciful indulgence. I tried hypnosis once and failed miserably, because my mind just would not relax enough to let in anything but my own controlling thoughts. I did not contradict the woman, who claimed she put me under. I am just brought up to be polite. Well, I was very polite, when I was younger. I don't have the time or nerve for that anymore sometimes. I try to keep it up. But it seems I am failing more often than I would like.

But there he is. Beautiful like in the movies I borrowed his image from.

"How is the writing going?"

I take the last step of the staircase with the cup in both hands. I get cold hands easily. Warming them on a hot beverage has something very calming about it.

"Shit, to be honest."

He laughs lightly.

I walk to my desk, put down the cup and sit down. I am annoyed. It is not funny. It is frustrating.

"What the fuck do you care?"

He looks amused.

"I do care", he says.

Why am I not surprised to see him? My rational mind tells me to at least question his presence. I don't.

"Why? So you can make fun of me? So you can laugh at the shitty sentences that barely made it out of my head, into the keyboard and onto the screen" - Damn, what kind of a weird sentence was that? Who talks like that? My face starts burning.

He just smiles, then shakes his head.

"Why would I do that? There is no reason to make fun." He looks at me and then at my computer. "I just can't wait to read what you will have to say." He leans forward, resting his elbows on his knees, puts his hands together and rests his chin on his fingertips.

"Tell me a story."

"I don't have one..."

"Of course you do. Everyone does. And you have a particularly interesting one. So lovely."

"How would you know?" I pull a face. I do so often these days. I have always done this, when I am annoyed with myself. A kind of mechanism to deal with my disapproval of myself. But it has become a more regular habit than before. I regret it immediately.

"I know you. I am in your head." He leans back and smiles at me.

"Tell me about Ella..."

ELLA

"What a beautiful baby", Ella thought. "So tiny." The skin still a little red and wrinkly. But what did that matter? This pretty face, the eyes closed. She had her little fist in front of her mouth and nose. The pitch-black hair. She was such a beautiful baby. It was hard to believe that only two days ago this beautiful creature had still been inside her belly. Kicking her day and night. Getting on her nerves. How much Ella had wished that her daughter would stop torturing her like that. Let her sleep. Read a book in peace. Always interfering. "Stop pestering me", Ella had complained, looking at her swollen belly and pushing the tiny bump down that she had thought had been a foot.

But it had been Emma's elbow. She was breech. Sitting on her bum. The lazy little cow. What a hassle. Already not doing as she was supposed to. Lazy, lazy. Ella was so annoyed. Peace. Please, peace, little one. Stop being a nuisance. But when the doctors had told Ella that Emma had to be delivered through a caesarian, she was pleased. No labour pain. She even joked with the nurses and flirted with the young doctor as they pushed her into surgery.

The painkillers made the breast-milk unusable. Still Ella dutifully put the pump over her slightly enlarged breasts every four hours. It was hardly worth the effort she felt though. Only drops. They did not tell her that the product of her small labour never reached Emma. Otherwise she would not have bothered after all. Never-mind the painkillers, it would have been too much of a logistic challenge to deliver the cups of milk drop-lets to the matching baby at the right time and keep it at the right temperature in between. Too much hassle. Formula and a strict feeding schedule were the only options to handle the daily intake of calories the infants in the ward required. It kept them quiet much more effectively after a maximum of two days as well. They got used to the schedule and asked for the bottle only when they were due after a while. Quick learners. Like clockwork. Very convenient. And anyway human beings need strict rules and schedules to function in society. To teach them early on in life made it easier for them to act accordingly later on. No damaging pampering and spoiling.

Ella pushed herself up in the hospital bed and reached for the Polaroid hanging from the bedstead. "So beautiful", she thought again. The nurses had kindly put up the picture over her bed for her to see just a day after the delivery. She was to recover from the surgery first for a couple of days before indulging in the life of motherhood. For a moment she had been convinced that something had gone wrong. Emma wasn't quite right. That's why she didn't get to see her daughter. The recovery, the peace and quiet, the tranquillity. Just excuses. They didn't want to tell her. But then the nurses had brought the picture. "A beautiful baby. See. Nothing wrong", the nurse had told her. "Stop being so squeamish."

All those babies. It had been a busy week.

Ella looked at her daughter again. Then she put the picture on the little table next to her bed with all those pretty flowers. She started to wonder if Emma would look as beautiful in person as on the photo, when she met her at the end of the week. Or would she be a disappointment? After all, people often look very different from their pictures. Would Ella be able to love the little one? A pretty face would make it easier. That was for sure. Ella had wished for a baby for so long. She had already given up, when suddenly she had lost her appetite for cigarettes. It was the first sign of pregnancy as it turned out. The pregnancy was fun. Finally no worries about being fat. The big belly looked weird, but gave her so much leeway at work and at home with her husband. Everyone took care of her. She was the centre of all concern and attention. She had loved it. Now that Emma had arrived, the big belly was empty. The prospect of losing her special status didn't appeal to Ella at all. She had rather stayed pregnant forever. But without the kicking. The empty flabby belly seemed to laugh at her. Mock her. You are not special any more. Get used to it. She despised it.

Well, a baby in your arms makes you special as well, Ella thought and pinched her belly with disdain.

She tried to get comfortable in her bed and picked up the book her husband had brought her yesterday. She was bored. The book was hardly a page turner. But the crossword puzzle was already done. Just a couple more days and Ella would be home again. Back to her life.

Ella had been a sickly child. The middle child of five. She could not go to school for quite a long time. Though she was never in any mortal danger, her mother always feared she would die on her. Even when Ella was fine again, her mother cushioned her against any strains. While her older sister had to help with the household and the younger siblings, her brother had to help their dad with other chores or get little jobs in the neighbourhood or in the nearby town to add to the family's income, Ella was left to her books, her passion for fairy-tales and other fanciful stories. She always found a shady little comfortable spot in the garden to stretch her legs, lean against a tree and read. The attic also had a wonderful warm corner in the winter next to the chimney, that she made her own. A little light. An old armchair and her favourite blanket. She got submerged in the world of make-believe. She fell in love with words, with all the pretty pictures that helped her form the world around her heroes. There was always sweetened tea waiting in the kitchen for her. A bit of stale left-over cake from the weekend, saved especially for her.

Her older sister resented her for it. While she struggled with school, the laundry and changing nappies on the youngest addition to their ever-growing family, Ella did not even notice the busy noises in the house. She did not see her mother's worn face. The weight loss that so worried her father. All she cared about was the opening times of the public library and whether mother would have time to take her there for a new pile of stories. The goblins and fairies, the pretty princesses and gallant princes, the gracious kings and evil witches... they all inhabited her everyday life intensely. They made her blind to the real world around her.

She felt it was most unfair when she was forced to leave her world of imagination for a couple of hours every day again. But after two years there was no arguing anymore that her health should keep her from attending school. She had hated those tedious lessons before her illness had allowed her to stay at home for a while. Take a most welcome break. She had never been so sick as to suffer much. Just weak enough to worry her mother and give her reason to spare her from scholarly hardship. She had been well again for quite some time. Yet her mother was not willing to let her go yet. She had lost a child a couple of years before. The girl had been three years old at the time. Her daughter had fallen out of an open window upstairs. She had been lying there in the garden for two hours before anyone noticed. No-one knew whether she died immediately. If she suffered. Broken bones. Pierced lungs. Drowning in her own blood. The doctor did not examine her. She was dead by the time he arrived. Beyond saving. What was the point. It would only torture the parents even more to know the details he reasoned and closed the case. Accidents happen. End of a sad unfortunate little story.

The neighbours had tried to console her. You have plenty more, they said. More than you can manage anyway. Don't you worry. It is all in God's plan. Everything happens for a reason. And if you want more... You are still young enough. They did not know, she had been asleep on the couch, when it had happened. Exhausted from carrying her youngest screaming baby around the house most of the night. It had finally fallen asleep, giving its mother the much longed for break. They did not understand that every child is special. Losing one, breaks a mother's heart forever. Having more children does not mend it. Ever. The fear of having her heart broken again and again drove Ella's mother insane. The guilt did its part. She kept seeing the most gruesome accidents in her mind. Fires consuming her beloved children. Evil men cutting their throats. Cars crushing their bones. Garden ponds swallowing them in a cold wet grave. Even a wet floor was a death trap, on which they could slip and snap their necks. A wobbly bookshelf could fall and bury the possibility of a long and happy life.

When Ella got sick beyond a harmless sniffle, her mother could not bear the thought of losing her. She was determined to keep her safe. Come what may. If she was the best, most caring mother in the world, God would not take another from her. He would not punish her again. Ella became special. A fierce mission. Her favourite child. Her only spoiled child.

Ella did not notice. She took the unearned privilege for granted. So convenient. It suited her. Her world of fairies did not have any room to register the hollow eye sockets on her mother's worried face. She did not understand her sister's resentment. Her brother's bemused comments. The absence of friends. She became unfit for the world that awaited her outside the cushy comforts of her childhood home. She resented the world and its demanding inhabitants for this unfairness, when her mother died. Poor baby. Poor Ella. So unfair!

ANNA

"Ella..."

The whisper suddenly brings me back into the reality of my house. My desk. Did I just say that name out loud?

My wrists are aching. My eyes hurt. I rub my neck. I suddenly realise it is already dark outside of my window. The milky foam on my coffee has long gone. The cup is still full. but cold. It is past midnight. I haven't eaten anything for hours. My tongue is dryly sticking to the roof of my mouth. What a horrible taste. I long for my tooth brush. I try to get up, but I have trouble to straighten my back. "Ouch! Oh for fuck sake!"... I need a pee. Desperately. I try to rush to the bathroom. My hair looks a little wild and sweaty. I pee. I brush my teeth. I get undressed and step into the shower. A few minutes later I go to the kitchen. Still a little bewildered. I pick up a bottle of water and down about half of it in one go. I feel a little sick. There is left-over pasta from yesterday. I put the pan on the stove and warm it up just enough to make it edible. A bit of grated cheese. Done.

I don't think I ever had a warm meal at that time of the day. I eat. I wash the pan and my plate. I drink more water, then rinse my glass.

I look up the stairs. Deep breath. Then I start to climb them. Determined. I half expect for him to be there. Sitting in that chair. Looking smug. So pleased with himself. So beautiful. I long to see him. But the chair is empty. Then I look at my laptop. For the first time I realise that I have been writing. I don't remember doing it. Not the way I remember putting down sentences, when I have been writing for the paper. But the cursor on the laptop is not alone anymore. The page is not empty. There are letters. Loads of them.

TUESDAY – A LITTLE LATER

I pull up the car to the parking lot. The name "Best Western" is towering in ridiculously big lit-up letters over the small hotel just off the main road. I am so grateful, they have their own parking lot. It seems there aren't too many options around for leaving your car overnight free of charge.

"Here we go." I sigh and give myself a little moment before I get out of the car. I grab my bag and my jacket. The package I shove underneath the passenger's seat.

The lobby is kept very simple, but friendly. Warm colours. Nothing too distracting. The girl at the reception desk gives me her most beautiful friendly fake smile. The kind of smile they have to learn at seminars. So clearly fake. Still. She is just trying to do her job well. So I smile back.

"Hello, welcome to the Best Western. What can I do for you."

"Hi... ehm... I have booked a single room... ehm... Anna Bennik..." I don't know, why I always stutter a little, when I have to deal with any stranger. Even, when I am entitled to talk to them. Say... as a customer. When I was still working for the paper that was never an issue. But then I was the journalist, not the person.

"Oh yes... here you are... Room number 16... That is just up the stairs and then to your right."

She hands me the keys. And a small questionnaire I have to fill in.

"Breakfast will be in the lobby here to the left from 6.30 till 10 a.m.", she makes an elegant hand gesture to my left – her right.

"If you want to get something to eat this evening, there are a few restaurants on the main street I can recommend, if you want me to."

"That's okay... ehm... I will just have a look around later and decide then. Thank you." I quickly scribble down all the information, that is asked for on the card. Then I give her an awkward smile, grab my key and mumble "Thank you" one more time, before I shuffle up the stairs, hating myself just a little for being so unnecessarily uncomfortable. She was perfectly nice after all. Not trying to strike up a conversation. Nothing. Just polite. Just all the information I might need. Nothing more. Perfectly trained to a standard welcome speech.

The room has a big soft bed, a lovely clean-looking little bathroom with a shower and soft white towels. The curtains are pretty ugly, but they look thick enough so they will block out the light from the street. There is an armchair. And of course Ben has made himself comfortable in it. An armchair without Ben doesn't seem to make any sense anymore. The thought makes me laugh. As if armchairs needed to make sense before Ben. Nevertheless, I am a little surprised to see him. There is no need for him to be here. I knew he would accompany me on this journey. A least for a bit here and there. I never thought about how much I wanted him by my side or not ... and where. He just happens to turn up. That is how it is. This is his nature. Or rather mine.

I am not sure, how it works. Do I subconsciously summon him? Is it his choice, when to be there? It probably has no real logic to it and it is idle to even try to find the mechanics behind his very being.

"What are you doing here?"

"You don't sound pleased."

"Sorry... I am. I am just not sure, what you are doing here."

He frowns a little.

"Company...", he says slowly. He smiles slightly as he gets up. He keeps his eyes fixed on mine as he walks over to me. He is tall.

He has to look down a little, as he stands right in front of me. My heart starts to race a little. He smells so lovely. His breath is warm and tingles on my neck as he bends down slightly to kiss my skin. His hands move up my back to my neck. I feel like my knees are going to give in any second. He moves away from my neck, takes my face lightly in his hands and looks at me. Just long enough to drive me a little wild with desire, when he finally moves in to kiss me.

The bed is a little too soft. The sheets a little too starchy. But his breath is sweet. His body so smooth. His touch so passionate. His whispers so infuriatingly arousing. For a moment he makes me feel desirable. So sexy.

It is getting quite late, when I leave my room to get some pizza around the corner from the hotel.

ANNA

There is someone new in my life. Fleeting. I have a feeling, he won't stay for long. It has been a very long time. My head has not produced a lot of inspirational material as of late. Not like before. There once was a time, when I was never without company. All those gorgeous men. Those little stories leading up to hormonal overkill. Those five seconds leading up to that most delicate touching of lips. Those images leading up. Always leading up. Never fulfilling.

That is the problem with porn for women, I guess. It is fulfilling. That is its sole purpose. There is nothing wrong with that per se. Sometimes, all I want is that wham-bham-thank-you-'mam shag. No fuss. No foreplay. Just get to the fucking point. Literally. It's quick. It is satisfying. And it takes no effort. No suffering. Just pure unadulterated sex. I don't even watch the "story-line". Badly acted. So embarrassing. Cringeworthy. No. Watching porn only makes sense to me, if I jump to the wild, rough humping – a few seconds later I am done and I switch it off again. Till the next urge for fast no fuss sexual relief. When I watch porn, I lose the ability for foreplay. I have to take a break. A long one. Wait for the humping images to fade. Porn has never been a prominent or regular feature in my life for that reason alone.

But this... This is much more delicate. More painful and frustrating, sure. But also kind of more satisfying. More desirable. The leading up to. The plot. The obstacles. The longing. Complicated. Fleeting. Slipping through my fingers of wild imagination before I am able to grasp it. It quickens the heart rate. Momentarily sets my loins on moist fire. Swooning. It can only lead up. The moment it starts to fulfil, it loses its charm. The hormonal spell is broken. If I am unlucky, for good. If I am lucky, I can conjure up an ever so slightly changed replay of the moment, those five seconds, for weeks on end.

They are images for masturbatory purposes. That is the simple dirty truth. Or the simple dirty origin of them. They are exchangeable and have been exchanged on numerous occasions. Just like Shakespeare's shadows. Faces to be cast for a single use. So many faces. Exchanged according to my fancy. Masturbation isn't just making love to a person you love, as Woody Allen put it. It is a fantasy acted out with your own hands. Sex is never as good as you imagine it whilst masturbating. If the fantasy is working. If you have found the right images. The big turn on. It isn't always the same. That would be too simple. Tedious. It changes all the time. And still... always the same patterns.

But it isn't as simple as to just imagine the faces and naked bodies. Caressing my skin, touching, kissing, shagging happily away. Horny expressions, ecstasy in their eyes. No. That would be too simple, too fast. Contrary to porn, I have always needed the story. The falling in love. The anticipation. The pain. The hurt. The hopes. The fear of being rejected. Just banging away isn't enough. Oh life would be so simple if it were. I envy men, who apparently can just picture a naked body and start rubbing with fierce and happy determination.

My fantasies need to be padded out. Have some, if not necessarily realistic, inner logic to it. But please... some ever so slight grounding in reality and possibility. I take my casting inspiration mostly from films. Naturally. You can watch them undisturbed. Take stock-images to be used later on. Casting in real life, your circle of friends and acquaintances can lead to terrible confused feelings, infatuations, broken hearts, broken misguided hopes, broken homes. It is therefore not to be recommended. At least not for this purpose. Actors are more safe. Distant. Non-threatening. They won't reject you. You will probably never meet them.

There are so many films that can kick-start the images in my head. The urge to just wander off to that place where falling in love and then ripping each other's clothes off is so quick, safe, fun and exciting.

No wobbly bits on my hips or bum to worry about. Gravity has not heartlessly altered the height of my once so perky nipples. Everything is just where I wish it was. A slightly improved version of myself. A little younger. A little braver. Lovely. And they all fall for me. I am not a breathtaking beauty they are all gagging for. No, I am still me. Just a little smoothed, I guess. Still full of insecurities though. Where would be the fun, if I knew, that I could have them. Excitement always needs the unknown. However fake it is.

I guess you could say, that I have a type. For sure it is not the beautiful men, that become the shining stars, the cover-boys. Perfectly toned bodies, shiny white straight teeth. The ones that the masses swoon over. Well, this might not be quite true. Once or twice one of my objects of imaginary affection has turned into a much admired and drooled over poster-boy. But they all start out as the nerdy ones. The sensitive, shy ones in the background. Uncomfortable. Burdened with self-conscious angst. Intelligent. Always intelligent. Some very funny. Tall, a little skinny perhaps. Sometimes a little menacing. The troubled ones. Always exceptionally talented and clever in their choice of projects.

Usually they play their roles perfectly for a couple of weeks of infatuation, only to hang around for pick-ups once in a while later on again.

The stories develop from basic ideas how I could possibly have met them. Usually a parallel life. My job as a journalist can come into play. Or a chance meeting, involving literally bumping into each other. Living abroad in New York, London. Being assigned an article in Toronto on a set. An accident. I have been in accidents involving inconsiderate cyclists who by means of fleeing the scene of the crime have got me close to the man of my daydreams by means of mere proximity, a bleeding forehead and fainting in their chivalrous arms.

One of my favourite scenarios involves me having pursued the dream of becoming a legitimate, maybe even good writer. Also any more marginal and maybe less glamorous job as floor manager or script girl at a production might get us close and get their attention. Common friends are also a possibility. But only if it involves moving in similar circles by means of line of business or place of living. See the above.

One story can stay around for a couple of days. Sometimes weeks. Be reinvented, re-imagined or retold every night or in quiet moments on the train, the bus or during a walk alone. Possibly leading up to a moment alone. Sometimes hours later. A little refined or changed every time. Lengthened or shortened. Bits and pieces. Sometimes told from the beginning or starting somewhere in the middle along the way. Constantly changing in details until they are used up and some new scenario or face finds its way into my head and fancy.

The need for an intricate and at least partially plausible story, instead of straight down to the rubbing-business between my legs is almost as exciting as the end result if it is ever achieved. I therefore don't mind that I tend to fall asleep before reaching my goal. That little explosion of imagined passion and real horniness.

Once a story is established I might just hop from one highlight to the next to reach that point of the first kiss, the ripping off of clothes, the merging of bodies, the sweat, the moans, legs wrapped around his body, whoever he might be.

They are still all there somehow. Once you fall in love with them, they stay in your heart. But they kindly make way for the next. No break-up. No bad conscience. Next please. See you later my love. Or not. Whatever. Whenever.

There has only been one who made it past the leading up to. Only one. He sits behind me in that big armchair every now and then. Knowingly smiling. Challenging me. Always challenging. Putting me under a strange creative spell. So far, all Ben ever did, was sit there. Smile and talk. He does not talk that much. But he ignites something with his few words. I get very annoyed with him. So smug. His smiles are so smug. As if he knows something about me, that I don't. This drives me mad. But it opens little boxes in me. Drags things out in the open and transforms them.

I always knew, I had issues. How could I not have? Given my life story. I did not expect to find them in those boxes though. I thought I had dealt with them. Dealt with them and cast them out. Moved on. Sometimes I am really stupid and naïve. I guess you are never really done with any of your issues. You just learn to either live with them or ignore them as best you can, while they sit in the corner, sniggering and sneering till you let your guard down.

Ben stuck around, it seems. We had such a great time together, when it was his turn. So rich in story. A companion beyond that first kiss. A partner more than anyone before him. Maybe it was just that time in my life, when I required something steady. Perhaps I got bored with just always leading up without ever getting there. With Ben I got there and stuck it out for a bit.

For a while now that space in my life had been empty. Pushed aside with work perhaps. Suppressed issues of all shades and forms. The dust bunny roaming the bedroom floor. Who knows. Until last night.

The space is visible again. And there he is all of a sudden. Willing to fill it. With his blue eyes. He is tall. So tall. Broad shouldered. Blond hair. Cropped short. He is far too pretty to fit into any idea or form of that category "my type". Too much someone you could cast as the handsome spoiled kid at an ivy league university. I am surprised, he showed up. There is no flaw on his chiselled chin. Clear skin. Symmetrical. The tight t-shirt suggests a body that spends a lot of time pushing and lifting heavy stuff. The look on his face is a little sad. A little tortured. The way us girls like the pretty boys. It is up to us to fill those eyes with the prospect of joy and excitement again. Oh what happy challenge! What could be more fulfilling, more self-esteem affirming, than to ignite happy fire in a tortured soul?

He walks out of the room with some other people. Leaving me behind on my own. One last look back. Our eyes meet. A thunderbolt through my beat-missing heart. Rushes of hormones. Then I am alone. Hot face. Unable to push back that smile. I walk over to the fridge in the corner behind the door. I am rummaging through it, trying to find some unidentified beverage. He walks back in. He takes off his jumper, when he turns to me. He is wearing that tight white t-shirt underneath. His eyes fixed on mine. Then he closes the fridge door while circling me. He is between me and the wall, when we lean in. Those beautiful blue eyes. Those curvy full lips slightly parted. I wake up.

Ben looks proud, when I walk up the stairs, coffee in hand. I forgot to brush my hair. I stop for a second. Barely looking at him. I don't really want to engage with him today. I have my five seconds to cling to. They will be gone soon. His image. Leaning in. Leading up. So fleeting. Let me hang on to him for just a little while. Five seconds.

WEDNESDAY

"Mum?"

A slender boy carrying a big backpack shoves the door open and runs into the room.

"Mum!"

He is maybe eight or nine years old. Brown slightly curly hair and so many freckles, that they seem not only to cover his face, but continue down his neck to the rest of his skinny body. His green t-shirt with some superhero-sign is far too big for his torso and dangles way down to his thighs. His trousers are ripped at the knee and covered in dust and dirt. He suddenly spots me and slows down immediately.

"Hello…"

He gives me a big friendly grin.

Before I can reply with much more than a smile, his mother shouts from the kitchen.

"I am in here, David!"

"Got to go", he says, motions to the kitchen and leaves.

I nod. But again, I don't manage to say anything.

The pumpkin soup in front of me is pleasantly hot. I have to add a little salt, but apart from that it is delicious.

The little bed & breakfast I chose for my second stop, isn't really a professionally run establishment. But rather a family home with three extra guest rooms at the top of the stairs and a big dining room on the ground floor. I did not know this, when I chose to take a right turn with my car and follow signs indicating an available room at the edge of the little town. There had been a lot of these signs all day. But I saw this particular one, when I had finally got tired of driving and thought, it would be a good idea to look for a place to stay for the night. I had only booked one hotel in advance of the trip, as I want to force myself to be spontaneous. Knock on a door and talk to people. Open up to sleeping arrangements, that have not been preplanned.

Apparently the family bought the house at a time, when they thought, they would have a lot more children. A huge family – that was the goal. A generous inheritance made a spacious home possible. But getting pregnant proved to be a little more difficult than expected. So after three children and fifteen years of always trying, they gave up, decided, that they were blessed with their healthy daughter and two sons anyway and should be content with what life had so willingly given them. Then they converted the extra rooms into guest rooms.

Mrs. Jodi Mazine told me all of this, when I arrived this afternoon. I never asked. But she was in a chatty mood and I felt too polite to stop her. She had some leftover cake, made a cup of tea and pushed me onto the patio. To relax for a bit after the long drive, she said. She joined me within a few minutes with a piece of cake and a cup of her own, plunged into a comfy chair right next to me and talked. She asked a lot of questions as well. About my trip, my home, my job, my family. I gave her short answers. She never pushed me on any issue though. For this I was grateful. But she told me about their life. Their home. Their guests. Their town. She laughed a lot and always smiled. Maybe it was the wonderful wrinkles in the corner of her eyes and mouth, that hinted at a cheerful disposition.

Her husband works for a nearby company producing office supplies of all sorts. Her kids are all in school. Doing fine. No big troubles above the normal, she said, shrugged her shoulders and giggled. She works a few hours here and there for a local law firm, but mainly takes care of everything around the house, the occasional guest.

"But they all help, when I need them to", she said beaming proudly.

I expected, I would want to go up to my room. Lock myself

in. Creep down for some food in the evening and again in the morning, before quickly leaving this all too cosy home again. I had regretted choosing this particular house, the moment I realised, how close I would have to be with the family during my brief stay. I had expected to feel miserable and uncomfortable. But nothing happened. I stayed on the patio. I drank my tea, ate my cake and listened to Jodi. The dreaded horror of a stranger over-sharing intimate information about their life, turned out to be a wonderfully entertaining afternoon. Even though the cake was a bit stale already.

After a while Jodi excused herself, patted me on the shoulder. Told me to make myself at home, stay a little longer on the patio and enjoy the afternoon sun. She had to go to the kitchen to prepare dinner for her family. Well, and me.

"Pumpkin soup", she suddenly announced . "Is that okay with you? I can whip up something else for you, if you don't like it. But I promised Eric that I would make pumpkin soup today. It is not the season for it, but it is his favourite."

"No – That's fine", I told her. "Please, no trouble on my behalf."

I stayed on the patio for a little longer, before I finally went upstairs to unpack whatever I needed for my stay.

After David had gone to the kitchen, it doesn't take long before the rest of the family arrives. Eric, 13 years old, I have been told, is not quite as cheerful and jumpy as his younger brother, but still as friendly in his 'Hello'. Helen, the oldest Mazine-child, a beautiful young woman of 17 years, even comes over to my table and introduces herself, before she goes to the kitchen, telling me to enjoy my meal. Mr. Richard Mazine arrives shortly after his children, but just in time to also catch me with the soup plate in front of me, welcoming me to their home.

I hear them chattering and laughing in the kitchen, which is located right next to the dining room. The family prefers the big sturdy wooden kitchen table for their meals, Jodi had told me earlier. It was just so much more convenient like that. And the kitchen provides all sorts of smells. Fresh herbs, vegetables, fruit, freshly baked bread, a fully stacked spice rack, which had led to many experimental dinners. Not all successful, Jodi had cringingly admitted. Thank God for pizza delivery, she had added and laughed. The kitchen opens to the far right of the patio and into the garden, that not only is filled with many trees, but has a big swing set as well as a dodgy looking tree house and numerous balls of all kinds of sizes for many different sorts of sports and past-times.

I do not mean to eavesdrop, but in the silence of the dining room, I cannot help but overhear the family's' discussions of what happened that day. Little incidents at school, a wonderful joke by one of Mr. Mazine's customers, running the track, reading Toni Morrison in English class, fighting with a girl named Cheryl about an article for the school paper, the TV show David is looking forward to this weekend and groceries, they have to pick up before the shop closes this evening.

"Our guest seems nice", Helen suddenly says, and it makes my heart jump. I did not expect them to talk about me. Even though it is a quite natural topic, since I am staying at their home.

"She is", I hear Jodi reply.

"Should we not invite her to sit with us", David says and I hear a chair being pushed across the floor.

I start to panic. I have finished my soup. I quickly down my glass of water, ready to get up and leave.

"She seems quite private, David. I already pushed myself on her enough this afternoon, I think. Maybe we should leave her alone."

"Nonsense", I hear her husband now laughing. "She can say 'No', if she doesn't feel like sitting with us."

"I will ask her!"

On my hasty way up the stairs, I can hear both boys jumping up and running for the door, playfully fighting over the privilege of who would invite the stranger into their family chat.

When I silently close the door to my room, I can hear Ben chuckle slightly. He is sitting in the big armchair in the corner.

There always seems to be an armchair. He gives me a strange, but very gentle look. It takes me a moment to realise, that it is hope, that is reflected in his eyes.

ANNA

He has returned a couple of times. But it already feels silly. Artificial. Clinging. A stupid teenage fantasy I feel far too old and, for lack of a better word, mature for. The pleasure is replaced by embarrassment. Ridiculous notions. If any man would behave like that in real life I would probably laugh at him, roll my eyes or walk away bewildered and annoyed.

That was quick.

When did I become so cynical?

Why can't I enjoy these little innocent fancies anymore?

I am so upset with myself. More so because the scenarios I came up with for him were very unimaginative. Very uninspired. No wonder the poor man never had a chance.

The weather is far too windy for a long walk today. I circle the kitchen like a caged panther... just not stepping so softly. A very old haggard panther with loose fur wobbling around its hanging belly with every stomping step. Not even my self-pitying imagery can escape used-up clichés.

I want to pull a face and throw some verbal abuse around the room directed at myself. But Ben's voice stops me. Well, not exactly. He isn't here at the moment. But he told me to stop pulling those faces. Be nicer to myself. I deserved it, he had said. I had pulled another face. I think I even stuck out my tongue at him. He had just looked at me in silence. Like a disapproving mother, who wants you to realise for yourself, that you are doing wrong, instead of scolding you.

"Fuck it...", I say – just a little too loud. I walk to the frontdoor. Coat, scarf, hat, shoes... Done. I am out of here.

Once you get used to taking a daily walk, you get addicted. I always fancied myself a lazy person. A couch potato, if given the choice. But I was wrong. A day inside makes me restless. I will never be the great outdoors person. Or sporty. But I need to walk. An hour or two at least or I go crazy. The wobbly dumb old panther lady that turns in circles just not to sit still for too long.

As soon as I am outside, I regret it. The wind is harsh and cold. It bites through the woolly hat into my ears. I need a destination. Quick. Some purpose. A pleasure walk through the fields is completely out of the question. A few leaves hit me in the face. One leaves a small scratch on the bridge of my nose. Great.

Purpose... Come on...

While I walk out on the street, in my mind I go through my fridge and my food cabinet. Bread. It's the only thing I could reasonably buy today. The only non-alibi-buy. Fresh bread. Maybe a piece of cake to go along with my coffee later on. Purpose found. Destination bakery. I am happy with my decision. I put my face down and labour through the wind towards the town centre.

As I open the door of the bakery about 20 minutes later, I regret my decision to have left the house today at all. For a split second I consider turning around and going back home without any bread. But it is too late. She has already spotted me. Sybil was a free lancer for the paper. Shoddy style, sloppy research, photos without any visible idea and to top it all... really bad spelling. But the paper hired her for the odd weekend event. Anything left over. Anything unimportant. Anything in desperate need to be covered, but no special attention to detail needed. A bit of editing usually did the job well enough. Sybil thinks we are friends by association. Old colleagues, who can share war stories. But I think she is embarrassingly untalented. And as unaccomplished people go... very self-assured and arrogant.

"Hello there", she immediately throws herself at me. Open arms for a pretentiously affectionate hug. Big smile. Kisses.

"Ooops... sorry", she laughs and starts to rub my left cheek. I assume, she planted lipstick there.

"How are you? I haven't seen you in ages. Oh that is right. Daniel told me. You are retired now. Hard to imagine. You old workaholic. I bet they miss their most busy bee there. But, oh well, life goes on. Everyone is replaceable. Though the quality of the paper must have gone downhill, since you left, right. Haha. She is such a perfectionist, this one (she points at my chest, while apparently talking to the woman standing behind her. Maybe a friend. Or another poor soul, whose friendship she just assumed.). Oh, how many times she just rewrote my perfectly fine articles. Oh well, water under the bridge. Do you still do some free-lancing? I haven't seen your name in the paper for a while. They still call me every other weekend, you know. Well, it is some pocket money, right? And something to keep me busy. Hard to imagine, you not writing anymore. Not sitting glued to your computer. Not rattling on on your phone. Busy, busy, busy. Asking all those questions all day. Oh, I bet you enjoy the quiet though. Haha. I heard you have a cute little house, with a cute little wild garden. Will keep you busy in the spring. You will see. Me, I grow lots of vegetables. So good to have some home-grown food. Wonderful garden. My husband likes it when I cook our home-grown stuff. But oh so much work. You hardly know where to start and where to end. Haha."

She doesn't seem to notice that I haven't said a word. It is my turn at the counter.

"Half a loaf of that bread over there, please." I point to that wholesome looking grainy thing in the corner. I put my money on the counter.

"Oh it was so nice to see you. We should totally meet someday for a coffee. Have a nice chat." She hugs me again. I mumble a half-hearted goodbye and turn to go. Just as I leave I can hear her half whispering, but without making too much of an effort not to be heard by anyone else but the woman next to her... "Always so grumpy. Sour-faced cow. Such a sad case. Lost her family, you know. Total workaholic. And now she has nothing. So sad."

Though I can feel the heat rising to my face, I pretend to be out of earshot. I haven't heard anything. I walk away.

I wish I had turned around and slapped her stupid face. Fucking ... face. Sybil... My cheeks are so hot now, that I don't really care about the icy wind anymore. Just get home. Kick something. Throw something. Scream. Just pull yourself together a few more minutes.

I reach my front-door. In the corridor I violently kick off my shoes throw my coat on the floor and kick the little cabinet in the corner. A searing pain shoots up from my toe to my leg. "Oh for fuck sake!!!", I am screaming now.

As I make my way to the kitchen I hear her laugh. So full of disdain.

"She looked right through you, didn't she." She crouches in the corner next to the couch. A can of gin and tonic in her hand. She laughs again. Sneering.

"The writer... you are a sad joke."

Rachel.

I too slip to the floor opposite her. Her sweaty face. The greasy unkempt hair. The blotchy skin. Tiny red veins spread over her cheeks like disorganised spider webs. The ones spiders make in labs under the influence of caffeine or cocaine. Eyes half open. When she starts laughing again, there is nothing left to hold back the tears.

"You phony", she spits in front of her. It was meant for me, but lands on her grimy shoes. She notices and wipes it off with her sleeve. There is also some spittle on her chin.

Chuckling to herself, she takes a sip from the can.

"Why do you get so upset?" She asks with that spittle-covered grin on her face. "It is not like she said anything, you didn't know already. No news. No shocker there."

"I am not a cow!"

"Really?" She laughs even harder this time. But it isn't a genuine laugh. "You aren't exactly the most cuddly warm fuzzy bear."

"I don't have to be nice to everyone. That does not make me

a cow..." I am doubtful.

Rachel stares at me. I suddenly realise, why she is called Rachel. She didn't have to tell me. Introduce herself. Just like Ben. I call her Rachel. Rachel Watson. Paula Hawkins' literary creation. She looks like Emily Blunt. The actress, who would inhabit the part in the movie following the best-seller success. The wreck on the train. The girl that had lost the plot and purpose in her life to be pulled back by a murder mystery. Destroyed by booze. Confused by gaslight. Such a tragic character. This is where Rachel was born. Now she is sitting in my living room on the floor, sipping her famous G&T from a can. And she added ugly features to her disposition. Disdain. A sneering quality to her distorted grin. Those faded eyes. It was the book I had devoured this summer. The one that stayed with me. Not because it was particularly good. It is a page turner for sure, but no literary milestone in any respect. But because I had a bit of time on my hands. Summer flu. The failed motherhood. The dead babies... They broke my heart. I don't handle harmed children in any story very well. Not that anyone takes something like that lightly. But I shut down.

She is such a mess. And yet – she is laughing at me. She feels superior to me. And I get the feeling she might be right.

"I am not a cow. I am not a sad story", I try to sound self-assured... Fuck... that didn't work out so well.

"So sad." She pulls an overly sad face and then starts her ugly chuckle again.

"ENOUGH!" I startle myself by screaming out loud, which makes her laugh even harder. Furiously I grab something next to me and throw it at her. The door stop hits the wall and leaves a dent. She howls in anger. Then she is gone.

ANNA

I think we were happy once. I am sure we must have been. Though I can't remember clearly. I don't trust myself on this matter. It might be my memories playing tricks on me. I push them away most of the time anyway. But I guess, we were happy. Not every day. But enough to justify the term.

I remember that I had been tired. A little worn out. A little annoyed. Yearning for some time alone. I had spent every day with my daughter. Every night she still woke me up once or twice. I just wanted some peace and quiet for a little bit. No calls for mommy. No food stains on my clothes. No tomatoey kiss on my cheek. No snot on my breast. Just me in a café. Or on a walk. Alone with my thoughts.

Nicolas had noticed the stress I was under and took a couple of days off. On a particularly lovely day, he suggested taking her for a trip. To a nearby town. Half an hour's drive. They wanted to visit the zoo. See the zebras and the koalas. Just daddy and his little girl. I was so happy about it, I practically shoved them out of the door. Kisses all around. "See you, mommy..." Have fun!

They had no chance.

The police told me the traffic jam came up too fast behind a bend. Between the two heavy trucks the family van offered no protection. No ambulance could have saved them. They wouldn't let me see them. The bodies were too mangled they said. Mangled. What a horrible word to use. I wouldn't be able to identify them.

I hope it was quick. Too quick for them to realise what was happening. No pain. No fear. No panic. But sometimes I have my doubts. I see my little girl's eyes filled with disbelief. Why isn't mommy here to make it all better. Nicolas helplessly watching her suffer, watching her die. Nicolas. Love of my life.

Tessa. My beautiful daughter. So stubborn. So cheerful. So gentle. So wild. So funny. So loving. So fierce. So...

She would be 31 years today. She will always remain three years old.

After a couple of weeks I packed away all her clothes. Her toys. Pictures of her. I couldn't bear seeing her, but not hearing her voice. Feeling her somehow always dirty warm little hands on my face. Smelling her hair. Hearing her breathing next to me at night. I put away all evidence that she had ever existed. Two days later I did the same with Nicolas. I left the town. I bought the house with the money from the life insurance. I got a job at the local paper. I became that journalist that remains in the office till the printers start rattling. The one that doesn't mind working on weekends and Christmas. It helped. I was just me again. I shut everything and everyone out. It worked. Most of the time.

It seems strange to pick a job, where you have to talk to people all the time. Make contact, when all you want to do is hide. Shut everyone out. An absurd choice. But there is no better hiding than in plain view. I never engaged with people. Never personally. It was the journalist. The paper. The proxy. The façade. It is so easy to hide behind a function. No-one suspects. You seem so open. So communicative. So involved. Always talking to someone. Never about yourself. So easy to hide. It also fulfils that tiny need for human contact that remains, even when all you want to do is crawl up into some hole and die alone.

But then... a vulnerable moment, a bit of misguided trust, a bit of gossip – and they all knew. My sad story. They had me all figured out. No wonder she buries herself in the job. Poor woman. No wonder she is so grumpy all the time. Have you noticed how she never talks about herself. She should get help, really. Denial is not the solution. I was the breaking news story for a whole week before they let me be again. Forgot my sad story. Most of the time. Tragedies have a way of creeping back up. They make for better gossip then nice stories.

I can smell her hair. That wonderful warm scent. Slightly milky. It washes over me. The memory violently grabs hold of me. Her laughter. Her smile. Her crying. Her clumsy cuddles. Her silly giggles.

My heart tightens. I can't breath. Then I start to scream. Howling. Crying. Sobbing.

TESSI!

ANNA

My head aches. The memory of last night is sort of blurry. Of course it is. Too much drinking. I have never had a lot of alcohol to drink. I don't like it. I don't like the taste. I don't like the buzz. I don't like the loss of control. I certainly don't like the hangover. I especially don't like drinking on my own. I don't see the point. It's just not my world. But it is Rachel's. Bloody Rachel.

I get off the couch. I did not even make it to the bed last night. My face feels weird. Dried snot tightens my skin like one of these thin facial masks you use to cleanse your face. I must have been crying pathetically for most of our binge. I am not even sure where the alcohol came from. I don't really buy any. Probably some decade old party left-over or present from someone who really has no idea what I like.

My tongue is fuzzy. The trip to the bathroom feels like it is taking hours instead of minutes. Bloody, bloody Rachel. Pathetic, pathetic, pathetic. Never, never, never again...

After some breakfast and a quickly brewed cup of coffee, I get upstairs.

"Good morning..."

I don't want to look up. I am sure Ben's look is judgemental.

"Mmhmmm..."

He starts to chuckle.

"That bad, huh...?"

"Hmmm..."

"You know what... I don't think you should continue Ella's story today."

I am surprised.

"Why?"

"I don't think, you are in the right state of mind for this today."

Now I am pissed off. How dare he... But he is right of course.

"What then? Take the day off and wander around the field? Take a trip? Watch T.V.? What?"

"I don't know. It is your time..."

Long pause. I am not sure what to do. I just stand there at the top of the stairs. Coffee in my hand. Looking over to my desk. I can feel him watching me. Waiting. My schedule has writing lined up for now.

"I tell you what", he finally says. "Why don't you sit down and write something completely different for a change. Something not so close to the heart. Something to take your mind of... you know... Something easy. An exercise of sorts. Some fan fiction. Something silly. Find some competition online and ... well... compete."

Fan Fiction. I snort and roll my eyes...

"Stupid, stupid...", I mutter.

But my muse is now really excited. He flings my laptop open and a minute later starts to search for writing competitions. Some inspiring nonsense. He is completely giddy at the thought.

I realise I am still standing in the same spot, when he turns to me, sparkling eyes.

"Found something..."

He turns the screen to me. It is a fan page of an actor I had a crush on.

"You like him, don't you?"

"What is the competition." I still act annoyed, but I must say I can't withstand his enthusiasm.

"You just fantasise about meeting the guy... Come on. It will be fun."

"This is embarrassing."

"I know!", he laughs. "That's why it is so brilliant!"

KAREN AND ANDREW

Karen just wanted two weeks to herself. No work. No friends constantly telling her that she needed a man. No parents worrying, that her life might be going in the wrong direction. No neighbours asking her for favours. Just a little holiday for herself. Nice little hotel. Lovely landscape for wonderful walks. Charming cafés. Restaurants with yummy food. Have a little swim. Have a read in the sun. Go for a movie. Nothing more. She had found this dreamy little town in the middle of Vermont that would serve exactly that purpose. And the perfect hotel to go along with it. She had sorted out a rental car as well to be independent of public transport. So when Karen sat at the airport waiting for boarding to start, she actually got very excited at the prospect of having two perfectly quiet weeks of "me-time". She was reading some easy-to-digest mystery novel, when she got distracted by the man opposite to her having a conversation on the phone. He sounded progressively annoyed.

While staring intensely at her book, she started to listen in.

"Ma... it is no-one's business... What do you care, what Julie thinks... Ma... please... No, I am not going to call her... Why? We broke up two years ago.... I know, you like her... I am not. Really. I will be fine coming on my own. Well, they will save money on the open bar.... Ma... I am not just going to invite some random girl, just so that Julie won't nag you... I don't care.... okay... you do that. It's not going to change anything.... Right... yes... See you in a couple of days... Bye."

Karen realised, that she had started staring at him and forgotten to use her book as a cover. When he hung up and suddenly looked at her, she quickly returned to the pages. But she could not concentrate anymore.

He looked annoyed and exhausted. The way she felt after most phone calls with her mother. When she got pestered about finding someone. When her mum raised all those concerns about her being alone. And it would be so nice to share life with someone nice. Someone nice... Karen hated that expression. Her mum meant well, sure. But what does that even mean. Someone nice. Just settle for someone not horrible. It wasn't that easy to fall in love. It just all depended on chance.

The man had put away his phone. He was very tall. Blond. Handsome. Dreamy lips. But very annoyed. The voice of the flight attendant came over the speaker. Boarding. And that was that.

ANNA

"This is stupid" … I am embarrassed… So I sit back.

"Keep going", Ben is gleefully leaning over my shoulder.

Sure… It is not really meant for publication. If any of my stuff even is. Just an exercise. But this is just plain stupid. Dreamy lips. Yuck! Where did that drivel come from. I am pulling a face.

"Don't pull a face." Ben didn't even look at me.

"Man, it's just not working. I am not one for fan fiction. It just feels very silly."

"What is so different? It's a story, right?" Ben looks puzzled.

"It's not just a story, is it. It is a fantasy about meeting someone unattainable. Someone famous. It's stupid."

"So?"

"It's juvenile…"

"But you have done this all your life." Ben genuinely doesn't seem to understand. "You dreamed me up."

"But I am not writing about that. It's intimate. It is too close."

"Why?"

"I don't know… It feels like… someone caught me masturbating…"

Ben raises his eyebrows. He seems to be intrigued. Or amused. Maybe he is just mildly giggly because I used the word masturbating. Who knows?

"But I always thought, that exposing yourself could make good writing. Show some truth. Raw genuine vulnerability perhaps."

"But that is sort of the point. It is not genuine. It is intimate, yet just not true. It is fanciful, but in a boring way. Just some masturbatory fantasy. If that is even a term. It brings about the desired effect for a short moment, but you really don't want to revisit it in a less horny moment. The same way you would watch porn to get off, but don't retell the poor plot to your friends afterwards." That was a weird comparison I admit, but I am desperate to make Ben stop pushing me. I am just not good at romance. It is hard to find unembarrassed truth in romance. Yet the greatest story ever told is "Boy meets girl". There is just no way around that truth. Not every writer can tell that story though without touching on kitsch. Sure a lot of readers love kitsch. But I am not sure I can write it without wanting to be swallowed by some sink-hole.

I could just refuse to follow Ben's instructions. I could just close my laptop and walk away. I know, I won't. But I could. Ben is very persuasive that way.

Ben shakes his head.

"Keep going. I want to know, where this is going."

I sigh and put my fingers back on the keyboard.

KAREN AND ANDREW

"It's not unusual" by Tom Jones was blaring through the large room. Underneath the music was constant chattering and laughing. The smell of sugary cakes and bland, but creamy food. Coffee, champagne, orange juice, beer, sodas, perfumes, already a bit of sweat. They all had their part in the mixture.

As Karen started nursing a slight headache, her eyes were looking for Andrew. He kept being dragged off by relatives. Constantly they were interrupted. Not one moment to themselves. They seemed all so happy to see her accompanying him. They did not know her. Not a lot of them made an effort to get to know her either. But they were so happy. All smiles. Relieved. Friendly nods. She was ambushed by some uncle and his wife for quite a while and learned a lot about life in Kansas, which apparently wasn't any different really to any life anywhere else in the country. But they had explained it to her anyway. They were nice. She could tell, that they had wanted to ask about Andrew. How they had met. Everyone in the room wanted to know. She wasn't really in the mood to offer the story. She left that up to him. She imagined that was all he was doing this evening. Telling their story. Most of it fake of course. But nevertheless... it was their story. They had agreed on it. Well, he had told it, and then had asked her to play along.

He just couldn't stand the nagging of his worried mom anymore. So he told her, he had met a nice girl. Someone he liked. Someone he got along with. Someone, who made him laugh. They had just met. They were both staying at the same hotel. They had been pushed together by a stressed out waiter as someone had forgotten to write down a big reservation and they didn't have enough tables to spare. So far so true. They might have ended up together anyway. A lovely little holiday flirt. Something casual. No pressure. But his mom kept asking him, why he wasn't bringing anyone to the wedding. Again and again. She just wouldn't let go. They were sitting in the restaurant of the hotel. His mom had arrived early for the big event and was staying at a lodge with her best friend. So he told their story. He just added a made-up kiss from the night before. Well, he just implied it. But his mother was happy. It would have been alright and no harm done, if Karen hadn't walked into the hotel restaurant a moment later to have lunch. And so their love story became official. Introduction to the future mother-in-law included.

The champagne tasted really cheap. Or maybe it had just gone a little flat by now. She couldn't find him. He must have been gone for at least an hour now. Constantly surrounded by someone wanting to talk to him.

Just before they had stepped out of the car to join the wedding crowd, Karen asked him, if he was ready to pretend being madly in love with her for a whole day and evening. It was supposed to lighten the mood. Make him laugh. Maybe jokingly cringe. But he had just looked at her.

"Not a lot of pretending there."

Then the groom had excitedly banged on the window.

Karen was tired. The weird excitement his remark sparked had turned into worry. What if it was just a joke? What if the moment had passed? She had fallen head over heals in love with him days ago, but hadn't been able to admit it to herself before. She had suddenly realised it, there and then in the car. But they had not managed to find any moment alone. And what would she say anyway? They were holding hands, they kissed, they smiled, whenever they were together... But that was part of the charade, right? She couldn't be sure anymore. And she did not want to kiss him for pretence anymore. It started to hurt. Nevertheless she was scared she might not get to kiss him anymore at all, if she confronted him about his remark. Admitted her own feelings for him.

She had been sitting there on her own now for a while.

Some slow song came over the speakers. She recognised it as "Falling Slowly" from the movie "Once". Just as Glen Hansard and Markéta Irglová went into the refrain, she felt a hand on her shoulder and then his warm breath as he leaned down. "Care to dance?"

The door had barely swung open, when he started kissing her and pulling her close. It had been difficult to contain their desire standing in the elevator next to that old couple. Holding hands and leaning just didn't seem enough. The desire seemed overwhelming. Everything had lead up to this. All that pretend affection. All those fake kisses. They were real now. They were overpowering. As soon as he had pushed the door shut, he started to undress her. Fumbling for the zipper of her dress, then pushing his hands through her hair. "I really haven't done this in a long time", he managed to whisper in-between kisses, before they fell onto the bed.

They hadn't talked during the dance. Just looked at each other ... and danced. There was not need to talk anymore. It was so clear. Then he had taken her hand and led her outside. Finally they were alone. And he had kissed her. Unseen by anyone. No need for any pretence. Yet...he had kissed her.

When Karen woke the next morning, Andrew had already gone downstairs. He had promised his mother to have breakfast with her before she left. He had told her last night. He didn't want to wake her. Karen got up. She couldn't contain her big happy smile. She went to the bathroom. After a long hot shower she stepped out. The mirror was steamed up... and it had a message written on it: "I love you."

ANNA

"Yuck..."

The ending might be abrupt. But I am tired and fed up with the story. I don't want to write anymore. I want to call it a day.

"Happy now?"

"Very...", Ben is grinning at me.

"Now go to bed", he says. I obey and get up. As I am making my way towards the bathroom to get changed, he adds: "Tomorrow, you'll be ready to face Ella again."

ELLA

Privatise. Privatise. If you want to keep some sanity, you have to privatise. Privatise. That is what Ella called her short cigarette breaks on the balcony. Her breaks from being a mom.

"Emmy, mommy is going to privatise", she told her toddler daughter before she shut the glass door behind her.

Emma knew, she wasn't allowed to disturb her mom now. Or there would be no point in trying to get her attention for the rest of the day. Emma understood. Trial and error. Or conditioning. Adaptation. Survival of the most considerate. Who knows what made her play silently during those moments, spread out during the day. What mechanics of survival made her function so unlike other toddlers.

"Privatise". What a strange word to use. But it made perfect sense to Ella. It was her private time. Outside her role as mother. Or wife. Or housewife for that matter. For five minutes at a time, roughly, she allowed herself to not be imprisoned by any role or definition. Caged by expectations. Breaking the cage. The cage. That is what life felt like these days. She never even considered that Emma might not go along with that arrangement. Why should she. Emma was so complacent. So willing to please her mom. She rarely succeeded. And Ella took little to no notice of her little girl's efforts. After she finished her privatised moment, Ella usually sighed, rolled her eyes and resented having to go back inside. To be unable to privatise some more. Read a book. Take a nap. Go shopping or do anything she wanted to do. She missed her old life.

She did her duty, though. Change nappies. Cook some food.

Sometimes just about edible. It is almost an art form, managing to burn fish fingers to a black crisp on the outside and have them still frozen on the inside. Emma ate them. Uncomplaining. The taste would never leave her for the rest of her life. It burnt itself into her long-term-memory. Forming a strong synapse. Just like the overly salted mushy peas and baby carrots. The runny mash. The horrible skin on the hot milk. The incredibly sugary red tea in the green ceramic pitcher with the red flower pattern. It formed the make-up of the motherly care and love she received. The nurture. Those were the moments Ella was truly there for her daughter. The moments she could have a genuine laugh at herself. Her inability to cook properly.

"Look at the mess mommy made again", Ella would giggle, while dropping the crumbled pancake or the lumpy tomato sauce with melted cheese with overcooked sticky pasta on Emma's plate.

"Never mind, honey – we will make some toast later", she would coo in a most amused mood, while walking back to the kitchen, still giggling to herself.

It put a happy smile on Emma's face to see her mother being silly. Such warmness. Who cares, what the food tasted like?

ANNA

I decided to go into the city today. Get away from my schedule. From the house. From the laptop. Ella has taken a turn towards my own issues. I did not intend for this to happen. It is too close. I needed to get my mind off it. Take a break. I could smell the burnt fish fingers. Taste the disgusting still frozen core in the middle of hard black batter. It had washed over me. All those bad dishes. The failed attempts at the stove. The disastrous results. The barely edible food. The emergency recipe of peeled potatoes with butter and cheese. The buttered bread, when everything else failed.

I am sitting in the bus, looking out on the street. Houses, shops, parks, people rolling by. I plan to go for some coffee. I have a book with me. I doubt, I will find the concentration to read. Find a café. Watch people. Put the smell of soggy rice pudding behind me. Go out for a really nice meal. Suffocate the stinky memories.

The bus pulls up to my intended stop at the city centre. I get up and walk towards the door.

"Why is that woman getting up", a little girl next to me asks her mother.

"I don't know, honey, you would have to ask her", a woman with a baby on her lap says.

I try to give my most open smile to the child, who is about three years old.

"This is my stop, you know", I tell her. "I have to get off here. Goodbye."

She looks startled. I guess not a lot of people react to her questions, but rely on the mother to handle everything. The woman smiles at me.

As I leave, I do not feel authentic. Very forced friendly.

"Sit down, Tessi", I hear the woman say.

The door closes. The bus leaves the stop. I am unable to move for a few seconds.

THURSDAY

It has been a wonderfully sunny day. Not too hot. A little breeze. Just perfect. The kind of weather that allows you to breathe in deeply. Close your eyes. Stop for a moment and feel the sun on your skin. That kind of perfect calming weather. I was lucky enough to be on the road. No rush. Just time. Nowhere particular to be. Not yet. Enough time. I covered a lot of miles on the first two days to be able to take it slow today. Wherever I found a nice path at the side of the road, I would stop and explore it for a bit. Enough to enjoy the view from the top of a lovely hill. Sit on a bench next to a meadow populated with 22 calmly grazing brown cows and their five calves. I watched butterflies. I tried to find a particularly loud cricket. I took Ben's hand into mine as we strolled through a small wood with a lake full of noisy frogs and blue shimmering dragonflies. I am usually scared of dragonflies for reasons I cannot explain. But today I just held Ben's hand and leaned against his chest, while watching those weird insects from a seemingly safe distance.

I stopped at a farmhouse café on the way for a simple lunch. Some apples for the road and the best milky coffee I ever had. I am sure that the chunky blue mug had something to do with it. As well as the fact that the milk was fresh from that morning. Or it was just the mood I was in. Ben and I talked for hours. Discussing everything there is to discuss between heaven and this earth. Walked in silence. Almost fell asleep, cuddled up on a bench next to a parking lot.

When evening came it felt like a waste of weather to turn to a house for accommodation and go inside. I just did not want to let go of the day.

"Camping."

"What?"

"There's a sign for a camp site", Ben points to the wooden sign ahead of us.

On other days I would have protested. Maybe laughed in his face. Looked at him in utter confusion. Or indignation. Camping? Seriously? Do you know me at all, man? But today, I just make a right turn and let the car roll down the bumpy road towards the camp site.

I don't own a tent. I am not for the outdoors. The adventure between open fires, shabby showers, cold feet at night, rustling sleeping-bags and damp clothes. I need my creature comforts. As simple as they might be.

The owner of the camp site has a few vacant camper vans for rent. So I just pick the one closest to the toilets. It has bedding and a bench that can be turned into a passable bed. A little fridge and a stove. Next to the van is enough space to park my car. The site-owner tells me about a grocery store just a short walking distance from the site, after he enthusiastically explained all the facilities to me. He realises immediately that he has a camping virgin before him and kicks straight into conversion mode. He is determined to turn me into the biggest camping fan in the world overnight and see me again every summer for the next couple of years from now on.

"You will fall in love with the perks and perils of this way of living", he keeps saying.

His almost childlike enthusiasm makes me laugh out loud numerous times, when he gets all excited about the gas bottle that turns the van into a "kitchen on wheels", even though the van has never been moved since it arrived on the site a few years back. The toilets and showers as well as the washing machine and dryer make him particularly proud. In-between overly complicated technical instructions he keeps telling me all kinds of mundane everyday occurrences featuring fellow camping enthusiasts. Even though every one of his stories is lacking any conceivable punchline, the anecdotes make him howl with laughter, just thinking about them, even before he comes to the apparently funny part. He has me in stitches when he decides I am now briefed enough to survive a night in the wild of his camp site and he leaves me to my own devices.

The trip to the grocery store turns out to be especially fun as it is surprisingly well stocked. It was fried fish, with cut up cherry tomatoes, white wine, tahini and cream sauce for dinner. And loads of freshly cut coriander to go with it as well as bread, still warm from some oven in the back of the shop. Ben rarely accompanies me on grocery trips. But I guess my giddy joy over the prospect of cooking in a camper van for the first time in my life, made him skip through the shop with me. Shaking his head in happy disbelief.

"Don't let this day end... ever." I cuddle up to Ben's warm body underneath the slightly stuffy blanket. "I really don't want this to end."

Ben kisses my forehead.

"The fish was delicious!"

"I know, right!"

I almost jump up.

"How come it never tastes this good at home?"

"I have no idea..."

Ben turns onto his side and props his head on his hand.

"We should probably not be so loud", I start to giggle hiding my mouth behind the blanket. "Mrs. Porthe might hear us."

The old lady and her husband are my neighbours. They own a camper van and spend as many days on the site as the weather allows them. Despite the fact that they have a lovely house right in the town, only ten minutes walk from the site.

"I still prefer the washing machine here. Makes the clothes smell really nice", Mrs. Porthe claimed.

Their puppy Geoff enjoys his freedom on the site as well and keeps running around, all excited by every new passing person or newly encountered smell. I have to admit, I have fallen a in love with Geoff a little bit. The moment he calmed down a little from his overly excited explorations of the perimeter, he decided to cuddle up on my lap and fall asleep for half an hour. The warm smell of his dog breath, the silky dark brown coat of this lovely labrador... I do understand now, why animals are used in therapy. He had the most calming and relaxing effect on me. And though I have read plenty about animal therapy, or whatever it is called, during my time at the paper, his effect on me took me quite by surprise. I have never seen Ben so happy and pleased. Sitting by the van. Watching me talk to Mr. and Mrs. Porthe at their camp fire, cuddling their lovely dog. Laughing, drinking, swapping stories.

"Let this day never end", I sigh again, cuddle up to Ben and yawn.

"I will hold onto it for you", he whispers. Or at least I like to think, that that is what he said. I think I fall asleep, before he is able to reply.

ANNA

I am pacing. I feel silly, but I am pacing. Back and forth. Ben is bewildered, I think. Or amused. I don't really know. I am unable to find words. Logic. Reasoning. But there is such turmoil. Maybe I need to pace it off to get to where I need to be. I really have no idea, what I am doing.

"What are you doing?" Yes, Ben is amused.

"I am pacing. Can't you see that?"

"I can see that. But why?"

"Oh, so the question isn't what I am doing, but why I am doing, what I am doing, right? You are misleading with your line of questioning."

"I was not aware, that there was already a line."

Stupid, stupid, stupid.

"Well, there are already two questions and..... and that would constitute a line... oh fuck... I don't even know what I am talking about..."

"Will you stop pacing, please", Ben is laughing now.

"No... I am not there yet..."

"Where are you going?"

"I have no idea to be honest. But I know I am not there yet."

"Why don't you go for a walk then? That would be less manic."

"No. There would be the danger of running into someone. Anyone. Too distracting."

I suddenly stop.

"Are you there?", Ben looks at me so amused, I want to slap him.

"Not sure..." I turn around to face him.

"Ella needs to go."

He just looks at me. I am unsure, what to make of his eyes. Those intelligent eyes are an enigma to me sometimes.

"Ella needs to go. Her character is not leading my story anywhere."

He is smiling now.

"That is not quite true."

"What do you mean? You don't look surprised. Do you know what it is that I'm trying to get to by pacing? Spit it out, man. My feet hurt and I feel very silly."

"She'll lead you to your heroine."

"I thought Ella was my ...for lack of a more appropriate title...heroine..."

Ben shakes his head.

I open my mouth, but I can't say anything. So I sit down. I am starting to realise, where he is going with this.

"Ella has only one purpose..."

"To give Emma a backstory. An origin. A mother. Someone who shapes who she is."

"Yes... I am sorry."

"No, no... that is okay."

I stare at him for a moment. He does not seem to mind. Being uncomfortable with anything just does not seem to apply to Ben.

"You needed to find Emma first. Your story is about Emma. Make her fall in love. Boy meets girl. The greatest story ever told."

Suddenly that moment of clarity.

"I can't image Ella falling in love.... in lust, well yes... in true love...no."

Ben looks pleased.

"You are right. She has to go now. She has served her purpose. But your story is not about her."

"I think, I will kill her off. An accident maybe." I did not expect myself to say that. And the words make my heart miss a little beat. I feel like I am about to start crying. I feel Rachel lurking somewhere in the house.

"Are you sure?"

No I am not sure. How can I be fucking sure about something like that. Being in my head, Ben should know that. It seems, Ben was betting on a different solution. Maybe, just phase her out of the story. Just shift the focus. Maybe... abandonment... kidnapping... a job in the CIA... No, that seems silly.

"Can I make a suggestion?" Ben has been watching me for some time. He can see the options, the possibilities of the story's shifts and turns in my eyes appearing and being swiped left.

"Sure", I am struggling now to keep a straight face. Keep my voice steady.

"Just start again. Tell me about Emma."

EMMA

"What do you think about Emma?"

"What?"

Christine rolled her eyes at her husband. She always did that, when he didn't immediately tune into what she was getting at. Robert was used to it. It wasn't dismissive, or insulting. Just impatient. Christine hated having to explain or elaborate on what she meant. She would have loved to be with a mind-reader – and hated it at the same time.

"What I mean", she said, putting an annoyed emphasis on the last word, "don't you think she would be right for Adam?"

"Oh, ...", Robert hadn't really thought about it and looked over to his friend, who was talking to someone at the bar. Adam had been miserable and alone for a long time, that was true. But Robert was so not in the match-making business, that he hadn't even given a thought to the idea of Adam being with someone new. For him it was always Adam and Madelaine. Anything else hadn't crossed his mind. Until now that Christine mentioned it.

"I don't know really", he now said. "I don't really know her that well."

Christine sighed and rolled her eyes again.

"I am sure, there is some potential there."

Robert frowned.

"How would you know? You know her even less than I do." That was technically true as Robert had met Emma a couple of times at Adam's stage show. She was really nice. Funny, intelligent, modest, interesting – and most importantly and not to be taken for granted – not nuts. Now that he thought about it, he realised that Adam had seemed very chirpy at those meetings. He had chatted much more, laughed and chuckled. Something he had rarely seen in his friend in a long time. At least behind the scenes. On stage he had been able, God knows how, to keep up his witty, quick-minded, cheeky, funny self as if nothing had changed.

Penny, who had overheard them, leaned in with an almost conspiratory smile on her face. "I am sure, that they fancy each other like mad."

"See!", Christine looked very smug.

Sally, who had been Adam's partner on stage once in a while, stepped next to Penny. "Who fancies each other? Gossip! Please, let's hear it."

"Adam and Emma – apparently", Robert was surprised to have joined in, even though he knew full well that conversations and schemes like that usually back-fired badly. Especially on him. He regretted it immediately.

"Oh, they are so lovely together, aren't they", Sally said with a dreamy expression on her face.

"Told you!", now it was Penny's turn to look very smug, enjoying herself immensely.

"How long has it been it been since he asked someone out? 20 years?", Sally wondered.

"22, actually – I think", Robert was annoyed with himself for saying that. As if it really mattered.

"Well..., we'd better do something about that then", said Christine in her typical practical matter-of-fact-voice.

"Hang on", Robert felt really uncomfortable about where this was heading.

"It is none of your business. If they want to be together, I am sure, they can manage themselves."

"Sometimes, people need a little push."

Robert knew his wife well enough to know, that the discussion was closed. She had made up her mind, that Adam's happiness was within the bounds of being achievable by giving him, well, a little push towards Emma. This worried him. What if

Emma didn't feel that way?

"It is Stephen's birthday next week. He wanted to get to know Emma anyway. You could get him to invite her to the pub or to his party", Sally suggested looking at Robert.

He hated being part of this. He hated plotting. And he hated asking Stephen for favours. Especially because Stephen would look right through it. There was no point though in mentioning it. Christine liked the idea. He could see that. So that was that then. Off you go little Robert, and do your wife's bidding, he thought and sighed.

ANNA

"Sooo... Emma and Adam." Ben smiled. "Boy meets girl. The greatest story ever told."

I have my doubts. So I start to pull a face.

"Don't!" Ben laughs. "Oh come on. How bad can it be. A little love story. Give Emma a racing heart. Not just a beating one. What is the story? What does Emma do, now that she is all grown up? Where do they meet?"

I sigh.

"Okay... I thought, maybe Emma became a journalist."

Ben looks surprised.

I tilt my head. Feeling caught in laziness.

This is easiest for me to write. I can just let the story do its thing without having to do any research on any occupation my heroine might have taken up. I can change it afterwards. Rewrite it perhaps. But journalist is an okay starting point.

"Write about, what you know...", I say and I feel very lame.

Ben doesn't look convinced, but he is not pushing it any further.

"Adam is a comedian, who has his own stage show. She is commissioned to write a piece about him. This is how they meet. At the theatre for an interview. Maybe... hmmmm... Adam is a divorcee. A little older than Emma. Troubled and heartbroken."

Silence.

"Or a widower?", I suggest.

"Hmm... maybe...", Ben is not satisfied yet.

"So now I need a reason for them to meet again. Socially

maybe? Like the party. I am not sure, I like the bumping into each other by accident on the street or in a store. Or... I am not sure about this."

"Try the birthday party and we will see..."

EMMA

Stephen had invited them to the pub for his birthday. Well, he wanted to throw a proper big party at the weekend. But he also did not want to spend his actual birthday on his own.

The Admiral Duncan. The cosy old pub was around the corner from Stephen's place in the city. They were regulars here. Emma was very excited to spend the evening with Adam. There were some other artists. All great comedians in their own right.

Nevertheless, she felt uncomfortable and self-conscious amongst the group. It didn't help that she had had to pull an all-nighter the night before as a colleague had mixed-up a deadline. Her boss had asked her to jump in at the last minute and write a story ten days before the actual hand-in-date. The night had been filled with desperate research. The old cliché... Journalism is literature in a hurry, she had thought, while refilling her cup with yet more tea at four o'clock in the morning. The story had to be handed in at 3 p.m. There were still too many gaps in the research to start typing and the quote-delivering-interview was scheduled for 9 a.m. No time to sleep. The plumber was due at 4 p.m.. The bloody toilet kept clogging up and her landlord had finally given in and done something about it, instead of sending her to the DIY store to get a plunger. And then they wanted to meet at the pub at 7 p.m. She also needed to pick up Stephen's present. Adam had told her about Stephen's weakness for a special Kenyan coffee. So the gift at least was easy.

As the evening got late the sleep deficit was finally starting to catch up with Emma. Even the most interesting conversation, or the funniest string of thoughts could not push it away anymore. It was such a lovely group of people. Each one a good reason to make a big effort to stay awake a lot longer. Just to enjoy their company. Listen to their stories. Engage in their ideas and arguments.

She had been surprisingly alert so far.

And there he was. Adam. Sitting right next to her. Their thighs touched, as there wasn't a lot of space around their table. But she had trouble to keep her eyes open.

"You okay?", Adam looked at her.

"Yeah, yeah", she said trying to pull herself together.

Damn it, she thought. You won't be in a situation like this every day! But she couldn't hide her fatigue from Adam. She could see that in his eyes.

"Just a little tired", she smiled.

What an understatement, she thought, forcing her eyes wide open. God, that must look freaky. Adam started to laugh.

"You don't say."

Then he leaned in a bit, so that the others wouldn't necessarily hear him.

"Do you want me to get you a cab?"

"No, I live quite close", she replied. "I will walk. Need the fresh air. Excuse me for a second."

She needed a little break, so she got up to go to the toilet. Maybe a bit of cold water over the wrists, a touch of make-up, resting her eyes a little, while sitting on the loo. Maybe that would be all it took to keep going for another hour or so. Maybe find the energy to enjoy the company.

"She is lovely", Stephen said and looked at Adam, who had followed Emma with his eyes as she walked off. Adam was taken by surprise by this comment. "What? Yes, she is", he said and looked at his pint.

"I don't want to meddle, but...", Stephen started.

"But you will meddle anyway", Adam finished, before Stephen could say another word and then looked at him with a more serious look on his face than Stephen had expected. Even Alan and Sue, who sat next to them noticed and stopped talking.

"Yes...", Stephen looked at his hand for a second to contemplate what to say next. "Yes, I guess you are right, I will meddle anyway."

A long pause.

"Don't", Adam finally said.

"I think, she likes you, you know.", Stephen said, ignoring Adam's annoyed expression. "And you should go for it. It is obvious, that you care for her a great deal. It has been a long time, Adam. What are you waiting for?"

"I don't just care for her, Stephen", Adam was getting angry at the old busybody.

"I am in love with her."

He had not expected to be so honest. But now it was out there.

"Not that it is any of your business", Adam was annoyed with himself for having revealed his feelings for Emma to Stephen. He liked the old man. But they were hardly close friends. The same could be said for Alan and Sue, who were now witnesses to the whole agony-aunt-scenario.

"Why don't you tell her?", Sue now joined into the conversation and Alan looked at him with the same question in his eyes.

"I really don't want to discuss this", Adam sighed. But they all looked at him, waiting for an answer.

"You are not letting this go, are you?"

Another pause.

"I am not sure, I am ready for something new. But I don't want to fuck this up."

"It's been four years, Adam", Alan said now. "Get back in the game."

"The game? That is the most stupid thing I have ever heard, mate."

Adam was visibly upset and started to check the door to the ladys' to be sure that Emma wouldn't suddenly appear behind him to hear the whole thing.

"He is right though", Sue said. "Get over it. People don't stay married for the rest of their lives anymore. They get married for a while, and then find a second partner... maybe at some stage a third. So move on to possible wife number two. Enjoy the freedom of dating again." It was supposed to sound cheerful. A little cheeky. Lift the mood. But it resulted in quite the opposite.

"Well, that's the thing", Adam said a little bitter. "I never wanted that. I wanted one wife and that was supposed to be it. If I do move on, I don't want to fuck it up. I don't want to date."

He got up and walked to the bar. Conversation over.

"Oh, that went well", Stephen sighed.

When Emma came back to the table Adam was still at the bar. That the welcome was a little awkward was an understatement. But Emma's attempt to bring some life back into her tired bones by means of cold water, eye-rubbing and make-up had failed miserably. She feared, she would fall asleep there and then. Possibly while still standing. So, she didn't notice.

"Oh, hello dear", Stephen greeted her making an effort to give her an innocent smile. Only now he noticed how tired she looked.

"Are you alright? You look very tired, if you don't mind me saying so."

"Sorry, is it that obvious?", she felt embarrassed, but too tired now to care about hiding it. "I have been up... well, about 38 hours now. It is catching up with me, I have to admit. I think, I will have to call it a day and go home", she said with a lot of regret in her voice, while scanning the room for Adam.

Where was he?

"Can I walk you home?", Adam was suddenly standing behind her.

The heavy weight of the sleep deprived long day made her skip a coy game of polite refusal only to give in the end.

"I will get my jacket."

She walked to the back of the pub.

"Don't say anything", Adam gave Stephen a warning look as he saw the smile on the man's face.

Emma returned.

"Oh, before you two go", Stephen started ignoring Adam's look.

"I am giving a small dinner party on Sunday. Very informal. Please no dressing up. Dirty jeans and t-shirt are welcome. But please, you are invited. Eight p.m. Adam, you do have my address, don't you. Just pick up Emma and bring her along. I refuse to hear a no from either of you. Lovely. See you there."

"Okay, thanks", said Adam, a little taken aback.

"And thanks for the lovely coffee, Emma. I am already looking forward to having a cup tomorrow morning", Stephen turned to Emma, got up and gave her a kiss on the cheek.

When Adam gave Stephen a hug, the old man leaned in to whisper in his ear: "You are quite a catch, Adam. Go for it. It is worth it. Even if I, a nosey old man, get on your nerves."

Then he gave him a reassuring smile that refused to discuss this any further and sat down to talk to Sue and Alan.

ANNA

Rereading my efforts at writing is a little embarrassing. Especially, because I can guess, what is coming next. When did I turn so kitschy? My story – if it can call itself that at the moment – sounds nothing short of a cheap erotic novel. But with pain. I'll never get to the point at that rate. But obstacles are so essential. Otherwise it just doesn't seem to be worth pondering about. A love that just happens, just is, is so boring. It needs the pain to become something. What would Romeo and Juliet be without their hateful parents? Without Mercutio being killed by Tybalt? Nothing. That's what it would be. The greatest love stories of all are born out of pain, misunderstanding and certainly the boy not necessarily getting the girl straight away. Leave it up to the very last pages to resolve the lovers' dance around each other before there is that all-solving wonderful kiss, briefly mentioned to wrap things up. And these are the light-hearted love stories. The dance, the doubt, the pain – it is all the more important to a good story.

"You are being boring", he shouts. He yawns demonstratively.

I am angry at myself, that I have chosen to write in the coffee shop in town today. I should have stayed at home. But I have stared more out of my window lately than onto my laptop screen. So I had decided to give the coffee shop another go. Have a change of scenery. The white noise of chattering around me. The loud hiss of the high-pressure air to foam milk. I had hoped to leave Ben at home. Out of my head. Have some me-time. Even though I know no-one but me can hear him, it always feels weird to have conversations with him in public. Even silent ones.

"It feels embarrassing, when I write about Adam", I think.

That is somewhat out of the blue. I am a little puzzled.

"What is so bad about writing about Adam?", Ben looks amused now.

Damn... I don't want to have that conversation with him. Not here. Not now.

"Nothing. I just... I don't know. Love just ... well... everything emotional makes you vulnerable. Sex is even worse. You expose yourself. Your fantasies."

"What about me?", he wants to know and he puts on his most seductive glance. "Does it feel embarrassing, when you are with me?"

I was not prepared for that. Especially because our fantasy happened a long time ago. But he seems to know I will blush at the sight of his seduction face. And yes... there it is. Burning hot. That is what my face feels like. Without fail. A little panicked and embarrassed I take a careful look around. Everyone around me is still busy chatting, drinking coffee, eating cake, reading – or whatever else they are doing. No-one noticed my bright red flaming face. Everyone is so self-involved and so noisy, that I just melt into the background.

"I..., eh..."

There is no point in lying to Ben. He already knows, how much I still love and want him.

"Yes, it does feel a little embarrassing as well", I admit. There it is.

He smiles and leans back. He is satisfied. At least for now.

"Give in", Ben says with a smile, that irritates me. "You know you want to."

I do. I want to give in to my silly fantasies, that make me sound like a teenage girl. Or a penny dreadful writer.

"Get him, girl", he says. "Again, and again."

Then he leans over slowly and kisses my neck. The heat rises from my loins up to my face. I am glad that no-one is looking. I am sure that I just closed my eyes and opened my lips for a second. Breathing a little too heavily to be just about the coffee in front of me. The café isn't noisy enough for anyone to hear it. It is just a split second. But I still feel caught and ashamed. His lips still linger on my neck. Gently caressing the skin just below my right ear. My heart pounds.

"Embrace us", he whispers with that sonorous voice of his that would be enough to forget, that I am not alone with him. "Love me. Get him."

I really hope, that no-one is looking over my shoulder to read this. Ben knows exactly where this is going.

EMMA

They had been walking in silence for a while, before Emma even noticed that Adam was a little absent-minded. She had been too busy concentrating on not dragging her feet, staying awake and not stumbling. But now that she noticed, it was very clear that Adam was deep in thought. Something was troubling him. The worry and concern, that something could be wrong, gave her a little adrenaline boost. Maybe he regretted offering to walk her home instead of staying with the others.

He is annoyed with me, she agonised, while she watched him. She almost walked into a lamp-post only noticing at the last second to make an unbalanced dance around it. That's when Adam looked up at her. His eyes were gentle, a little anxious. They had been walking quite close together. He looked down and reached for her hand. She had been in love with him from day one. Yet never daring to hope. But she wanted him badly. Loved him even. And now he had reached for her hand. They walked a little closer together. Fingers intertwined. His finger-tips gently caressing hers. And then he suddenly stopped. Pulled her close to him. He took her face between his hands and looked at her for a moment. Then he leaned forward and kissed her. Very gently and careful. She returned the kiss. Giving herself over to him completely. Pressing her body against his. Feeling his warmth. He smelled so nice. He tasted a little bit of lager. He released her slightly to look at her again.

"I am taking advantage of your sleep-walking", he said with a little grin.

"Am I dreaming? Or is this really happening", she asked.

He laughed quietly and brushed a strand of her hair to the side with his finger.

She hadn't noticed that they were already in front of her house. The realisation made her jump a little. What to do? She didn't want the evening to end. Especially now. But she wasn't sure how long it would be before her eyes would finally give in and fall shut. He made the decision for her

"Get some sleep." He started to push her playfully towards the door. Then he kissed her again. Slowly. Infuriatingly slowly.

How can I say goodnight now, she asked herself, when Adam suddenly released her, gave her the most beautiful happy smile, turned around and left.

ANNA

"FUCK!!!"

I take the little stress ball that I got in the mail as a publicity present from some new yoga studio or meditation gym or whatever the fuck else it was, and slam it against the wall.

It makes Ben, who I miss by just a couple of inches, jump. Especially, because the little ball bounces off the wall and is now happily flipping around the room finally smashing into a vase on the shelf. It is inevitable. The vase falls down and shatters. I never liked the stupid thing. It is too small for a proper bunch of flowers and falls over, when you put anything in it that is heavier than a daisy. Now it is gone. Bloody vase problem solved. Nevertheless. Now I feel stupid in addition to my anger.

"What the fuck was that?", Ben looks at me with wide eyes.

I can hear that little cackling drunk laugh from afar. I close my eyes and push it aside.

"Fuck off", I try to direct it at Rachel, but I look at Ben instead. He is here after all. Rachel is not. Not quite yet anyway.

Ben looks at me and waits. He knows, that I will talk eventually. So what is the point in arguing. I am so predictable it is infuriating.

"It is shit!", I say and point at the screen as if what I am saying could be mistaken as referring to anything else.

"Why?"

"They kissed!"

"So?"

"It is too early. He just said, that he does not want to fuck it up. And minutes later he changes his mind and kisses her?

Bloody unlikely! Also... it is too quick."

"And a changed mind and a quick kiss are bad?" Ben looks irritated.

"It is too easy. Not enough pain. Not enough obstacles."

"Then change it and do not throw balls around. It is your story. Change it, if you don't like it."

I stare out of the window. It is a little windy. The old willow's branches are dancing back and forth. A few clouds.

Where would they go from here?

Jane Austen quite rightly always ended her novels with the wedding. Not the wedding night. Or the marriage for that matter. It is right there at the very end. Always. Just after the declaration or realisation of the love between the heroine and the hero. We all know almost from page one, that they are meant to be together. But it has to wait till the last page. They have to find out the hard way, complicated, ever-so-twisted by funny misunderstanding circumstances. Just a little afterthought. Oh, by the way, they got married in spring. What a lovely wedding. Everybody was there. Thank you. The end. Jane Austen, the queen of romantic comedies. Every story in that genre is a copy of Lizzy Bennett and Mr. Darcy. No wonder the hit "Bridget Jones's Diary" followed her example. Novelist Helen Fielding didn't even hide that fact that there is no point in pretending otherwise. This is the ultimate love story, that is worth telling. Boy meets girl. They fall in love. But for a long time they are too stupid, self-involved, modest, scared, taken, prejudiced, proud or something otherwise to realise it and actually do something about it... Till the last page.

There is only one other love story that is worth telling: Boy meets girl. They fall in love and do something about it. But because they are too stupid, self-involved, scared, taken, prejudiced, proud, terminally ill, bound by contradicting loyalties or something otherwise so their love is doomed to fail, they are star-crossed lovers who die or fuck up their relationship in some other way. Everything else is boring old life and ends up in a contented marriage and everyday mundaneness. But it doesn't make for good story-telling. Obstacles are the key. Obstacles that have to be overcome in some shape or form.

"Fun fact about Jane Austen...", I force an enthusiastic smile at Ben. "She loved novels. The art form of it. You can tell by the way most of her characters treat novels – or literature for that matter – who they are, or what Austen deemed important about them."

"Really?"

I am not sure Ben is all that interested.

"Yes... Emma, Jane Austen's, not mine, draws up reading lists with all the right choices. Her heart is in the right place. But she is too all over the place, too ditsy, you could say, to follow through with anything. She never reads those books. Catherine is overly romantic. She therefore reads Ann Radcliffe's Gothic novels and almost falls for the wrong man, instead of seeing who is right for her. Mr. Collins, thinks novels are a silly, female past-time... nothing to be taken seriously. He therefore is one of the most silly unsympathetic characters. And her best character of all times, Lizzy, loves novels for the pure joy of reading them. The way you should read them. The same goes for most characters. Their attitude towards literature defines them as characters."

I pause and lean back for effect. I am always quite proud of that observation. Though it isn't really anything new. I keep bringing it up, whenever I want to impress someone with my knowledge of early 19th century literature.

Ben is not that impressed. Awkward. I look back to the laptop screen.

"This is shit", I mumble.

I hear that laugh again. I think, Ben might have heard it as well. He turned his head to look over to the stairs. Or maybe I am just imagining things.

"Maybe just let the story roll along for a little bit further. See where it takes you. It is not your big happy ending yet. I, for one, would like to know about the dinner party at Stephen's. Come on. Take me there and if you don't like it, you start again."

Ben tries to give me an encouraging smile, and then looks over to the stairs again.

"I need a coffee first", I say. I get up and walk down the stairs to the kitchen.

I half expected Rachel there. The disdainful laugh. The drooling spittle on her chin. But the kitchen is empty. A ray of sun hits the kitchen table. Dust dancing.

Maybe it is the smell of the coffee. Maybe... Ben. Images of a garden party started to fly through my head. I sigh.

"Okay, Ben. Party time, it is."

EMMA

The little wood behind the house looked beautiful in the warm September sun. Almost no wind. Still warm enough to be very comfortable in just a breezy t-shirt. Not the heat of the previous month anymore that made you break out in a sweat if you were silly enough to indulge in as much exercise as lifting your arm to get something to drink from the table in front of you. It smelled strangely and wonderfully of sweetly rotting fruit from the orchard across the brook.

What incredibly silly picturesque scenery, Emma thought and started laughing to herself. She had never taken Stephen to be such an old-fashioned romantic. But there it was. His beautiful little cottage taken from a magazine. The old intellectual and the countryside. Well, country… just outside London. He had his apartment, smack in the middle of Soho. But he needed a breather on a very regular basis, he had told her when they arrived. And yes, the house was stuffed with lots of gadgets as Stephen was a bit of a self-professed nerd as much as a bon-vivant and allround know-it-all. Nevertheless, a couple of horses in the background and the picture could have been published in any magazine promoting the beauty of country life.

She was still shaking a little. Taking deep breaths. Closing her eyes. Her heart raced. She looked back at Stephen's garden and the terrace where all the guests were socialising, eating, chatting easily, laughing and mingling.

"Small dinner-party, my ass!", she thought and took another deep breath.

There were at least thirty people. The unnerving part. She

knew most of them. Though she had never met any of them in person before. It is a very strange experience to follow someone's career on the television, the literature circle, the theatre or admire their writing style in renowned newspapers or magazines for years. To know someone's face better than those of the friends you have known for years, just because it was acceptable to stare at a picture in a magazine and study a person's face. Any of your friends would think you were losing it, if you were to look at them for longer than a couple of seconds at a time.

And now there they were. In the flesh. The stars from all kinds of public walks of life. A famous bunch of funny, talented and clever people. Stephen had called. And they all came. Apparently this happened every year. Stephen just took advantage of his beautiful home and of the professional position, which allowed him to meet the most interesting people in the business. And now she was there too. It felt like a very weird dream and even then she was sure, that she would even then feel like the odd one out.

Stephen had dragged her off for a couple of minutes just after they had arrived to chat to her.

When he had let her go again, Adam was nowhere to be seen. She was supposed to mingle. To get some food. To make small talk. All breezy. As the food seemed to be the least frightening part of that list she had gone over to the buffet and filled a plate without properly looking at what she had stacked on. Though everything turned out to be delicious it was a strange assortment of things that didn't really go together. Sweet and spicy. Smoked and covered in whipped cream. Once she had eaten everything - eating was excuse enough not to converse with anyone, she felt – she clung to her empty plate for a couple more minutes, feeling ridiculous and slowly panicking. She had already eaten too much to go back for a second helping immediately, so she had no choice but to let go of her safety plate. Without anything to hold onto, her palms started to become sweaty and hot. She became horribly aware of her arms and had no idea in which position to hold them. Everyone was already engaged deeply in chatter and Adam was still nowhere to be seen.

There was a little shed at the end of the meadow behind the house with a little bench behind it. It was a little hidden from sight, which served her purpose perfectly at the moment. It had already been over half an hour that she had been sitting there not knowing how to make her way back into the jolly party crowd.

"Hello there."

Robert popped his head around the corner of the shed.

"Oh good God, you startled me", she said shaking even more than before.

"Sorry. I didn't mean to", Robert gave her that uncomfortable look, that he was so famous for and which she thought had just been an act.

"I just thought, I'd better have a look how you are, since you disappeared to the newcomers' hiding spot, as it is famously known by us in the know, and hadn't emerged for quite a long time", he gave an encouraging smile. "Oh yes, we all know this spot so well. We have all hidden here at some point or other. Well, some of us anyway. I have this theory that Stephen put it up for exactly that purpose. To give newcomers a chance to hide, when they are first invited to one of his soirées. But then again I might be wrong and it is just lucky coincidence and Stephen has no idea that this can be very intimidating."

Robert looked back to the others with his arms crossed behind his back.

"I can still not bring myself to find this normal", he said.

Gratefully she gave him a smile.

"So...? Is it really obvious, that I'm hiding? I might be just admiring the view", she tried to be jokey about the whole ridiculous situation, but was quite aware that Robert wasn't having any of it.

She had met Adam's colleague and friend a couple of times before, but they had never talked to each other alone. She had always liked him though. Even before, when she had just known him from his work. He was a very different comedian than Adam. A lot more cynical and angry. Posh and a little repressed. Cultivating a sad loner image. Very well-educated and a little neurotic. But very sweet and kind behind the camera. He was also very quick-minded and wonderfully creative. Someone who genuinely enjoyed his work and the people he worked with, even though for his public image's sake pretended not to.

"It is hard to believe, that any of the people present here ever felt the need to hide", she finally said. They all looked like they belonged.

He started to chuckle.

"Oh, you have no idea. Penny and me had to fight over this spot for a couple of years. She is quite feisty. We then decided to form an alliance and just talk to each other instead. Adam hid here, I believe, five years ago. Full-on panic attack. But not as long as me. He was found by someone after only a few minutes and dragged out. They almost started a really weird fight. One year we ended up having a little separate party behind the shed with about five or six people."

"You are making this up just to make me feel better", she gave him a very strict look.

"Yeah, well, maybe", he now sat down next to her on the bench.

"So... tell me, why you are here and not on the terrace, preferring solitude to our delightful company."

"I don't have to tell you. You already seem to know", she said. But he just waited. So she sighed. It wasn't just, that she felt like a fish out of water amongst them. It was also Adam. He had told her that he loved her. And she hadn't had time to respond to it. She felt awful about it. He had told her very suddenly. There was nothing planned, anticipated about it. It just came out of his mouth. Seemingly surprising himself. They had been standing at the curb waiting for his friend Sandra and her husband Ned. They had arranged to share a cab with them to go to Stephen's party. They had met up just outside her apartment as it was closest on the route to Stephen's.

She and Adam had been standing there for only a couple

of minutes. Completely undecided whether or not they should kiss again as the other party guests could turn up any minute now and be witness to the first moments of their relationship, affair, love. Sandra was a wonderful person, but a horrible gossip. So Adam seemed not to be too keen to get caught in the act. Even though he didn't say this or ask her to keep it secret for now. So it was just looks, awkward, evasive conversation, nervous smiles. Then he suddenly had just touched her hand lightly and told her.

"I love you", he had almost whispered.

He didn't even look at her, when he did. He breathed in sharply as if a little in disbelief at what he had just done. Her face went hot. She wanted to tell him, that she loved him too. She wanted to kiss him, hug him. Laugh, cry, tell him to forget the party and drag him up to her apartment. Into her bed. But she didn't. She didn't say any of it. At least not out loud. There was no time.

He still hadn't looked at her, when the black cab pulled up next to them only seconds later and Sandra rolled down the window.

"Hello, you bastard", she trilled and grinned at Adam. "Get in!"

The cab ride had been a little unreal. The others had been chatting cheerfully away and Adam had obliged. Joking, small talk. He had not looked at her too much. She had smiled along, trying to look at ease. She even tried to be a polite part of the conversation, whenever one of their two companions had asked her something or directed a comment her way. No trace of the romantic tension between the two new lovers. It had to be postponed.

Once they had arrived they had been swept away into the chaos of the party as they were late. Probably the last to arrive. Stephen had immediately dragged her off and Adam was ushered by someone over to a group of people discussing something about dog racing. Or maybe horses. She couldn't be sure. There had been too much loud chattering in the room to make out exactly what they wanted. And then he had been gone.

The confession of love without any reply was hanging in the air. Every dating convention would deem the declaration too early. There had just been one kiss. Well, two. But only a minute apart. No date yet. No sex. Not a lot of alone time so far. And still he had told her. Some couples seem to find that phrase even too early after a couple of months of dating.

Dating. What a stupid word. So restricting. So bound to strange rules that had nothing to do with falling in love. But still she had not answered. And it had been about two hours since Adam had exposed his feelings for her. Still he had no idea how she felt about him.

Robert still looked at her. Waiting for an answer. She wouldn't tell him about Adam. That was for sure. And anyway, officially she wasn't hiding from Adam. She was hiding because she couldn't find Adam and felt like she just didn't belong here. At least that last part was something that she could tell her empathetic companion. That was what he expected. Surely. It was quite clear after what he had told her. And anyway, it wasn't a lie. Not really.

"It just feels so surreal to see all those people here", she finally said. "Those people can't be real, if you know what I mean. They are supposed to stay on the other side of the screen or inside the paper. You are not supposed to meet them. They are not supposed to cook with water or go to the toilet. And they are certainly not supposed to talk to me", she said. "That holds true for you too, by the way", she said, slowly starting to relax at the idea, that she was talking to Robert. "I just don't belong here."

"What makes you think that?", he said and laughed as if she had just said the most ridiculous thing. That took her by surprise. She had thought it was quite clear, why she didn't belong. She wasn't famous. She wasn't successful.

"You are wrong, you know", he said and smiled. "Most here have read your articles. They all wish we could write like you. You have a gift. You cow!" He now fell into one of his famous mock-rants, where he got all heated about an argument, too mundane to actually get so worked up about. "Have you no shame, I ask you. If you now get up at a karaoke and turn out to be a good singer as well, I think one of us is going to tackle and choke you. Please, for the love of God, tell me that at least you have two left feet and keep falling over even at the slightest attempt to walk in a straight line across the street." He pushed his hair dramatically back in the side-parting as he usually did at the end of a rant. Point made.

"Fuck off", was all she could say, which made Robert burst out laughing. She couldn't help but laugh as well. Ice broken. Anxiety attack resolved.

ANNA

"Keep going..."
Ben has left his armchair. He is standing behind me. Reading.
"Keep going...".
I turn around to look at him. He smiles reassuringly.
"I don't know, where to go from here..."
The branches of the willow are swaying back in forth. A peaceful dance. The sun being caught in the leaves.
"Bring them together and see what happens..."

ADAM

Adam put the key in the lock. But then instead of turning it and going into his flat he stopped and put his head against the door.

"Fuck…"

What a stupid way to end a really messed up day. Well… On the surface it wasn't all that messed, sure. It was all perfectly pleasing. The party, his friends. Emma being there. It sounded nice. A wonderful summer's day as well. All lovely indeed.

"I am such a fucking idiot!" It caught him somewhat by surprise that he had said that out loud. And so he looked around quickly to check no-one had been listening. It was very unlikely, considering that it was now already well after midnight. A little embarrassed and annoyed he turned the key and walked into his flat.

He had known very well that he and Emma wouldn't have a moment to themselves once the cab had turned the corner to pick them up. He had been to one of Stephen's parties before. Many actually.

They had kissed once. Yes. And yes, she had returned his kiss. Nevertheless, he should have at least kissed her again before jumping in like an idiot screaming "I love you!". Well, he didn't scream. Obviously. But he felt he might as well have.

"What was I thinking? Nothing, Adam. As usual…"

She had said nothing. She had no chance to. Bloody perfect timing. But what would she have said, if she did? He took out his phone and contemplated sending her a message. Taking it all back. Haha, just joking. Good one…

She must have been horrified. Adam hadn't been able to shake that feeling that he had really fucked it up. Whatever chance there was, that they would be together. He had scared her off.

The drive back in the cab had been very awkward. Sandra and Ned were jolly and drunk. Talking no-stop. To themselves, to him, to Emma. Not requiring any answer or interaction from them. Emma had sat quietly, sometimes giving him a strange look that he couldn't quite read. It was the same look that she had been giving him all night after he had found her again amongst all the guests.

He was looking at his phone again. Unsure about what to do next.

He started typing... "I am sorry about earlier. I shouldn't have said, what I said..."

"Oh sod it..." He deleted it again and threw the phone on the sofa. He then went to the bathroom to brush his teeth and get ready for bed. No point in staying up for much longer. He would just torture himself with regret.

He did love her. More than he thought he would. Losing Madelaine had scarred him more than he cared to admit. He had been so convinced they would grow old together. A love like that could not be destroyed by anything. Surely. So strong.

After losing her he didn't think he would ever be able to love someone again like he had loved her all those years. He was convinced he would love her till the day he died. And that was what he intended to do. A love like that happens to you once and that's it.

And then... Emma. He had loved her almost instantly. Been drawn to her. Every minute that he spent with her made him fall in love even more deeply than he had thought possible. And now... he had blown it.

He had meant it, when he said that he loved her. There was no doubt about that in his mind, heart or gut. But to spring it on her like that had been stupid.

"Stupid! Stupid! Stupid!"

The poor girl. He felt miserable.

He put on his pyjamas and turned to the bedroom when he heard a faint knock on the door. And then again. This time a little louder.

When he opened the door, his heart stopped for a second as he saw Emma standing in front of him. She looked very, very nervous. Before he could even say anything, she stepped forward, put her arms around his neck, pulled him close and kissed him. Clumsily. Then she let go again and stood in front of him. Nervously looking at her feet. He breathed in, trying to say something. Anything.

"I love you", she suddenly said and looked up.

"All day, I wanted to tell you. All day I was on the look-out for a little moment, when I could tell you. Or show you. But there wasn't any. I just couldn't stand it anymore. I had to see you. I am sorry for barging in here like this in the middle of the night. But...", she paused. She was shaking a little. "I love you", she whispered.

He realised he had just been staring at her for what seemed to him to be far too long to be appropriate. Adam took her hand, led her into the flat and closed the door. They stood there. Looking at each other. Both nervous. Shivering. It was the first time they had been alone. No more obstacles. No more reasons to be apart. No more boundaries. Then he stepped forward. The kiss was very different to the one on the day before. First gentle, but then hungry, longing.

"I love you so much", he whispered and then kissed her neck. She pressed herself against him. Breathing heavily already.

It didn't take long before they ended up in the bedroom. Pieces of clothing forming a scattered line marking their way.

ANNA

"Oh what a happy little fuck! Silly romantic goose!"

Rachel must have thrown up. The smell on her breath is horrible. She leans over my shoulder reading the last sentences.

I slam the laptop shut. I feel caught. I am shivering with anger and embarrassment.

Rachel starts laughing, then she loses her balance and stumbles backwards just to fall to the floor on her bum. A strand of greasy hair ends up half in her mouth. As she tries to balance her upper body into sitting straight up, she wipes the hair clumsily off her face and then breaks out into hysterical laughter.

"Whoopsie daisy... - fallen over..."

"What do you want?" I try to stare out of the window. Concentrate on the willow. The dancing leaves. The sun is already fading.

"Nothing", Rachel tries to look like an innocent little girl. Astonished big eyes.

"Nothing really." She can't keep it up. Maliciousness creeps back into her look.

"As you have nothing to give. Nothing good anyway."

Though already on the floor, she almost falls over again from laughing.

"Oh what drivel. I love, love, love you." She makes kissing sounds.

"When did you become so pathetic. So lazy! This is shit!!!"

Her eyes are blazing now. I am not sure it is joy or anger. Maybe both in a twisted mix.

"Get used to it! You are shit at this! This is drivel and it will never be anything else. You are nothing! Certainly not a writer! Do you fancy yourself someone, who can write such a wonderful book, that the famous invite her to their party? Admire her? Think her brilliant? Dream on! Pathetic!" She is spitting again. A little puddle on the floor. I think she has also pissed herself. The smell is getting piercingly strong.

"I am not Emma", I whisper.

Rachel falls over again. Giggling.

"Oh yeah, I forgot. It's Emma, not you. She is fictional."

She is on all fours now, struggling to get a grip on the floor.

"Dream on! They will never admire you. They will never even know you exist! They haven't known you existed up to now. You are far gone, past your prime. Your local journalism has never meant anything to anyone. You are nothing. No-one cares!"

"I am not Emma", I say again.

"Of course you are not! It couldn't be more obvious. The journalist. The brilliant woman. Desired by a man. Of course you are not her. But do *you* know that?"

I can't swallow. I can hardly make out the leaves on the willow anymore. It is getting dark.

"I am not Emma..."

ANNA

"Get up!"

Ben is slowly coming into focus as I unwillingly open my eyes.

"Get up!"

He is angry. I can tell. He is trying to hide it. But he is angry at me.

My knuckles hurt. I remember. I took a punch at Rachel. I hit her cheekbone. Fucking cow! I hope I broke it. Probably not though. I have a bump on my forehead. Just a little to the right. I hit my head on the corner of the desk. She pushed me. There is blood on the floor. Not a lot. But distinct. I assume it is mine, as Rachel's blood wouldn't leave stains. But who knows.

"Get up..." His voice is annoyed now.

"Okay, okay... Leave me alone."

"Why?"

"What? She started it. Can't a woman have a little brawl?"

"I don't mean your ridiculous catfight", Ben says.

He is worried about me. The blood. The bump. The broken skin on my knuckles. Oh and my fucking back. As I try to get up, the hours of lying on the wooden floor have taken their toll.

"Aaaah... for fuck's sake...that hurts."

"Why did you delete it?"

"I don't know what you are talking about..."

"The pages... why did you delete them?"

I remember. Before I punched her... I started to believe Rachel. I hated the writing. It was stupid. The leading up to the kiss. I didn't feel it. On the contrary. Oh the shame. I should have punched her straight away instead.

"Fuck!" I put my face into my hands.

"You could have rewritten it, you know. No need to throw it away."

I get up now.

"Coffee... "

When I get back a few minutes later, I have thrown some water in my swollen face and brushed my hair enough to get rid of all the tangled bits. I found a big bruise on my thigh and one on my bum. There are a few more somewhere spread across my body, I am sure, but I haven't checked thoroughly yet. I have no idea how they got there. The coffee in my hand, the wonderful warm smell... I am starting to feel a little more sane again.

Ben is still upset.

He pushes the laptop back into its regular position and opens it.

"Start again...", he says. "Get them together. Give them a chance. Find their story."

He is making an effort to calm down. Deep breaths. Closed eyes for a moment. He leans down and kisses me on the neck, then turns around to sit down on his chair. Yes, it is his chair now. I don't think I will ever sit in it ever again, I realise. He has claimed it for himself.

"Okay... start again."

FRIDAY

I have lipstick on my lips. Brownish dark red. I have always liked the shape of my lips more than any other feature of my face. They are nice. Full. A little curvy. Not as full as they used to be. But still. Nice. The colour used to go well with my hair. It has too many grey strands now to highlight or mirror any colour. I stopped dying it ages ago. Or putting on lipstick for that matter.

Sure there is an element of laziness in the lack of make-up in my daily routine. Sure. I have to admit that. I did not feel the need to put any on. I did not want to attract a mate. Of any capacity. Ben does not require make-up. He saw beauty without any surface.

I try to claim though, that abandoning make-up was a conscious decision. In a way that is certainly true as well. Just not purely that. A feminist decision by the way, if pushed to put a label on it.

Women are so conditioned to believe that their worth is directly linked to how they look. The more beautiful the better. Making an effort to maximise your superficial beauty is part of any woman's success story in most walks of life. Well, sometimes beauty might work to her disadvantage as well. Usually in the workplace, but not restricted to it. Depending on the field or position she wants to be taken seriously in or on the people she wants to be taken seriously by. But in general, as it is suggested by magazines, films, friends, family and people no woman should give a flying fuck about. One way or the other, surface determines a woman's life and recognition.

Improvement begins at the hair salon, continues with the

perfect peeling, the right foundation product, the right shades of red on your lips, that convey your personality and ends with a magically relaxing manicure, that we actually convinced ourselves is just for our own benefit, instead of presenting our perfectly managed nails to a possibly interested male. Again the nails are a window to your personality and an expression of your worth in this world. And then the perfect outfit to finish the surface personality. This idea of female surface is so deeply rooted in our collective consciousness, that taking the bins out without a nice outfit and make-up for the leisurely occasion seems to be a social faux-pas of the highest order. You should have a make-up style for every occasion.

Whether you go out to a fancy dinner, a wedding, the grocery store, the office, outdoors, even your couch or the swimming pool. There is a style for everything. And if you are not up for it, you let everyone down. Especially yourself. No matter how far we have come in terms of rights and equality, the surface, the idea of beauty being required, stubbornly defends its place, extending its influence via polished social media filters, putting even more pressure on young women.

Even the rouged reality is of course very different indeed. And if you try to look at women's faces on the street instead of looking at your phone or staring into a magazine, you will very quickly see that she does not have the fitting look for every occasion. None of them do. Those that do look like women in magazines seem strangely out of place. Most of the time you just grab whatever is not in the dirty clothes basket, fits, has no holes and is more or less comfortable. Women in the real world are quite practical. Even at the office. A pencil skirt or a sheath dress are the exception to the rule. The oh so perfect make-up is not so perfect after all, has white lines on the edges because staying in bed for ten more minutes was preferable or because the kids made a quiet minute in the bathroom simply impossible or maybe because you just have no clue about applying make-up and your book is so much more interesting than an intensive course by means of a YouTube tutorial. We are too practical to style ourselves when we take out the trash. Nevertheless, magazines, social media and all the rest of what is buzzing around in this media-driven world are busily trying to undermine the practical self-image of women by suggesting that naturally every (!) woman is making an effort, to follow the newest trends in fashion, make-up and all that goes with it and most importantly obeys those rules. Seriously, every woman! Granted those working in fashion probably do follow the trends. But they most likely slump down on their couch in the evening wearing nothing but baggy comfy clothes – not the stylish baggy comfy look with the fitting make-up and the tossled up-do. Instead they're like the rest of us: unkempt hair, blotchy skin and the super-comfy pants, with the hole on the inside of the right thigh, which you don't want to chuck out, because, well... no-one will notice, so who cares? The suggested dogmatism put forward by cooperations, the effort put into trendy beauty as dictated by the media influences women in their sense of self and worth in order to make money – and perhaps also to lead them to believe that they can only fulfil or reach their true worth if they bow to those unreachable maxims of beauty and really put an effort into satisfying all those trends. Only then can the prince see Cinderella's worth. Only then will the ugly duckling, which had justifiably been pushed around and bullied, since it had not made any effort, turn into the beautiful swan that is deserving of respect from all. There could not have been a crueller game invented and played in order to keep women permanently just a little below men. Because women are convinced that it is their own fault if they are not successful in which area of their lives it may be. Infamous presidential daughter and walking image of a successful business Barbie, Ivanka Trump, therefore advised women first up to buy a new dress, if they want to be successful in their office jobs. Wearing new clothes would change their own confidence as well as how their colleagues and bosses perceive them. Doesn't it say that the devil's biggest success was that he made everyone believe he did not exist? The biggest success of the man's world is to make women believe they can be successful if the just deliver on the right surface. And we women have really eaten that one up. It doesn't matter how progressive we are. It doesn't matter how much we don't give a shit about what others think about us. The conviction that beauty, which can be reached only through our tireless effort, is the key to our success and happiness, is embedded deeply within our belief system. Consciously or not.

Sure, men have fallen victim to manscaping and fashion more and more of late as well. But you would never hold it against someone with a penis, if his regime of grooming did not go past the regular shower and the occasional facial shave. The social values of men and women manifest themselves as interior and exterior.

I tried to free myself from this. I reasoned that since I had no interest in attracting a male or pleasing anyone with my exterior, putting on make-up for my own benefit, so that my face would not make me jump in fright every time I walked past a mirror, was just a silly notion. Make-up, the surface is always for the others. To please them. To convince them you are worth their while. I did not need or want their while. So I gave up.

I kept up the basic hygiene of course. Brush teeth and hair. Shower, wash. Change clothes. Smell nice. You don't need to annoy or intrude, even if you are not out to please. Use a care product, when my skin felt dry and in need of some cream or so. But make-up disappeared unused in some remote corner of my sponge bag.

Today I am glad, that I grabbed the bag without having a look at its contents. Without sorting out what I thought I might need and throwing out anything superfluous.

I stand in front of the mirror. My freshly washed hair is nicely brushed and pleasantly arranged. The make-up is flawlessly, though subtly applied. A bit of powder to take away the shininess on my excited face. A little rouge, though my cheeks seem to be red enough. My racing heart seems to supply enough excitement to my bloodstream. But just in case. A tiny bit of light eye shadow to highlight the shape. I was never able to get a good hold of eye-make-up. It is just not something I ever mastered. Even in my most superficial years of prancing around like a clownish show pony. So just a little touch will have to do. And then... there are the lips.

I am actually very happy with the result. I smile at myself. I feel beautiful. I look beautiful. Even to the most critical eye and considering my age. I look beautiful. I am a little rusty. But my make-up applying skills are still there. Readily tucked away somewhere in my brain for that moment they are needed again.

The reason. It is so obvious, that it is embarrassing. I want to attract a male. Not any. I am not suddenly desperate for any male attention. A particular male. Martin.

So, yes - his name is Martin. I met him today.

I was very reluctant to leave the camp site this morning. Even sad to say goodbye to the puppy Geoff. I patted his silky coat one last time, before he jumpingly ran off, apparently excited about some mouse he had heard in the corn field next to the camper van. The camp site owner gave me that knowing triumphant look. He knew he had won me over. He knew that look I gave the old camper van that had been my home for about 14 hours. The place I had felt so happy in. In Ben's arms. So happy. Where I cooked that wonderful fish. My one-night-neighbour, Mrs. Porthe gave me a warm hug.

"Have a safe journey, honey", she said and smiled at me as if we had not met yesterday but had known each other from years of camping together.

Ben waited for me in the car.

I thought I was sad, when we drove off. It startled me quite a bit, when I caught myself smiling broadly, sitting behind that wheel.

Ben had watched me closely, as he so often does. He started laughing loudly at my weird jump.

"Surprised that you are happy?", he asked not holding back with his chuckling.

"Yes, to be honest..." And then I burst into laughter as well.

After a while we calmed down enough to talk. But we kept bursting into fits of giggles again and again.

I raved about the food from last night. That beautiful dog. I retold Ben stories of our camping neighbours, while Ben watched me with an almost loving look on his face. I was so wound up and excited that I even feel the need to tell him about the sun, that had decided to shine warmly that wonderful evening.

"It is still there", Ben said looking out of the window at the beautifully lit landscape flying by.

"Oh yes." I was beaming.

"Oh by the way, I have some ideas for a few stories", I suddenly said.

"Really? Go on. Do tell."

"Just rough ideas. I want to write a children's story about a dinosaur that loses his home, a big beautiful cave, in an earthquake. It is one of those herbivores with the long necks. A diplodocus, I think. He likes flowers. He was out collecting flowers in a meadow, when it happens."

Ben looked extremely amused now, but I wouldn't let that get me off track.

"He now has to find a new home and meets all kinds of dinosaurs. Maybe even a mammal. But it is all in vain as they are not compatible in their needs. Maybe a family of carnivores wants to eat him in-between. Or he accidentally destroys the home of a much smaller dinosaur. I don't know yet. Maybe he has to spend a rainy night outside or something. Anyway... at some point, when he has already almost given up, he comes across a meadow with a lot of beautiful flowers. And in that meadow there is a diplodocus girl, picking the flowers. After a conversation filled with gender-prone misunderstandings – oh the hilarity (Ben can't stop laughing) – they decide that it would be a good idea to move in together and share their love of flowers. The happy ending."

Ben was still laughing and I giggled along.

I told him more ideas. One about a serial killer and his potential new victim moving towards each other, directed by destiny. One about some farm animals that find the rooster dead one morning and have to deal with the murder mystery. One about a small town dealing with an alien invasion happening far away in the big metropolis. But they can't be sure as all communication has broken down.

"You know what. I don't care anymore. I have put on paper what I needed to get out of my system. The drivel and the good stuff. The pain and the sex. I feel incredibly free. I can write whatever I want. I can create any silly or wonderful or evil character I want and make them do whatever I want. I just realised that there is no bloody need to prove myself to myself anymore. I got that book out. However good or bad it is. Who gives a shit. It is out. It took all that rewriting. All those new starts. Over and over again. Now I got it all out. Shat it out. Told a story. Now I can tell any silly one I fancy. For myself. For you. For any stupid moron out there willing to pick up a book. Everyone."

I shouted the last word and made a grand gesture, that was suppose to include the whole world out there.

When I looked at Ben, he was not giggling anymore. He had tears in his eyes. And a big smile on this face. Even more so. His look was so full of love and maybe pride, that it made me shut up immediately. It took a lot of effort to bring my eyes back to the road. So I pulled over and stop the engine. I took a big happy breath. Then I turned to Ben and kissed him.

"Thank you", I whispered.

It took a little while before I was able to start the car. And a few minutes more, before I found my voice again. For hours we talked about possible stories. Tossing around ideas and characters. Some too silly, some dark. Sad stories. Happy stories. Funny stories. Fantasy. Horror. Love. History. More dinosaurs. Explorers falling in love with beautiful natives that don't speak their language. Animal stories. Coming-of-Age. Artists struggling to find their place in life. Political thrillers. Whodunnits. Real crime. Nothing too silly, too absurd, too serious or too kitschy not to be considered.

I realised there and then that the world of literature was open to me. I was open. I was free. And I had all the creative power to do with my characters whatever the hell I felt was plausible and fun to write.

Fun. What a strange concept to have crept up on me after all those years of carefully constructed hidden away misery, well-managed and low maintenance and well-constructed contentment. Fun. That was all I needed now. Fun in writing. Maybe even fun in life.

Ben and I spontaneously decided to follow a sign for beautifully advertised cabins next to a picturesque lake. And even though most of them were booked by families, senior groups, single traveller and newly-in-love couples, there was one cabin still free, smack in the middle of the compound. I would have usually longed for the far end of either side to avoid contact if possible. But this fitted my newly found thirst for possibility. Throw myself in the mix of people. Talk to them. Oh well, or at least not look for a hiding place or an excuse to leave as soon as they signal an interest in talking to me. Let's not jump too giddily ahead too much.

The compound has a barbecue set in the middle of the cabins that has been built into a semi-circular shape around it. It became clear very quickly that it was set to be used that evening and everyone was invited to join and make a meaty contribution. Once again, I was told about the shopping possibilities near by, which I immediately put into use.

Then I met Martin. He has piercingly blue eyes. Full silvery grey hair. And wrinkles in the corner of his eyes. I assume he has lead a happy life with loads of reasons to laugh. Wrinkles around the eyes suggest that. Right? Happiness and laughter.

I talked to him briefly, when I got settled in my cabin. Carrying in my bag. Well, he talked to me mainly and I smiled at him. But I am a little smitten. I admit, that it is probably the previous mood in the car that sparks an interest in the opposite sex more than his sexual prowess in itself. But he is single and roughly about my age. So I started to rummage through my sponge bag for that long neglected lip stick and all the other products that have started to develop a bit of a dusty smell about them. I even found a small bottle of perfume, that I used to like. Not too old to have faded or turned into something nasty.

Martin does not know me. He does not know that the lipstick has not been used for at least 15 years. Or even longer. As much as I can make my characters do whatever I want. I can reinvent myself. Pretend for a few hours that I am that picture perfect of accomplished femininity. Wear my leisure clothes like I have carefully chosen and assembled them with an outfit purpose in mind, instead of just by grabbing the first comfortable thing in the bag. I can hold myself like a lady. I can be charming. Seductive. Funny. Anything I want. If I fail... Who cares, I guess. I will never see him again after my time at the cabins.

I look at myself in the mirror again and pull a kissy face. Ben puts his chin on my right shoulder, wrapping his arms around my belly.

"You smell lovely."

No snarky reply. No weirdly pulled face. For once I take the compliment without belittling it. Just for once. I know, I am beautiful. Even without the make-up. But I make an effort in the mating ritual of us silly humans. I ruffle up my most beautiful feathers and I come out feeling like the most fancy bird in the flock.

Ben kisses my cheek lightly.

"Have fun tonight. I love you!"

I smile. I definitely do not need that rouge.

"Thank you. I love you, too!", I am not sure, if I said it out loud. Ben does not care either way.

EMMA

A week in the life of Adam, the comedian, the actor. A little window, an insight into who he is. Intertwined with interviews, reports from the stage show and life on the road. Some quotes from other comedians Emma was supposed to get at an after award party to top it all up. An unusually busy week. Well, an unlikely week to be honest. The paper had asked for Adam to play along. The editor wanted all these aspects of his life in the story. So they just had to pretend and meet a couple of times in the course of two months. The interviews were to happen in between shows, meetings and the party. She was suppose to follow him around and scribble down any detail, any quote by him or colleagues, or fans for that matter, that she thought might be usable in the final piece. That was the idea.

Already on the first day, which didn't have any other meetings or shows scheduled at all, she had enough material to fill a small book with her notes. They had met at his office to talk, to get to know each other, to get her most important questions out of the way. It had been his idea to arrange for this extra day before letting her play fly on the wall in his work life. Just to make sure, that if push came to shove, he would be able to focus on his work instead of having to answer questions at any given break he would get in between high-concentration moments. Basically he wanted to make sure that she would not annoy him. He needed to be in control of the situation. But he had sold it to the paper as an extra exclusive day for an in-depth-piece.

Nevertheless, Emma looked right through it, but met with him to work through all the points she had prepared.

This first meeting took about three hours of firing question at first and then slowly slid into a more casual chat. That was her interviewing technique if she had the luxury of that kind of time with someone. Get the facts out of the way and keep talking till they felt comfortable enough to actually share some personal, emotional or funny stuff, which they wouldn't if it was a fast-paced interview. She listened a lot, interrupted as little as possible and dropped a line of inquiry if she felt her interview partner didn't want to go there. It was not exactly a technique that was favoured by most journalists. It was actually frowned upon, as it was seen to be more professional to ask hard questions, jump in and cut off answers that tried to down play things or lead away from an uncomfortable truth. But usually Emma got better results than the hardliners in her job. People were on the look-out for the tough questions. Politicians especially were often highly skilled in obscuring them and giving vague answers that couldn't incriminate them in any way. If people started to trust you though, they let their guards down after a while. You just had to make sure to keep the interview going.

In Adam's case that wasn't hard as he was in no hurry to finish it off. He had reserved the day for exactly this. However much she needed or wanted to know, she should get it off her chest in advance. Even if it took the whole day.

The first hour or so was spent just ticking off things that she already knew through her research. She just wanted fresh quotes and made sure that all the sources checked out. She had read his book, watched and read all the interviews she could find. They talked about his childhood, his early wish to become a comedian. His idea that it was an unobtainable goal. How he got started, his first gig, his first break, his idols, his colleagues, his passions, his work ethics. She didn't try to find any new angle or information that wasn't publicly known already. She didn't ask him about his family or his marriage, his private hobbies or his friends outside the business. She knew he liked to keep this private. He was protective of it. He felt that it had nothing to do with his job and was therefore not really of much interest to the public.

He obliged patiently and even told her a few anecdotes that she hadn't read about yet. He was not only surprised to see how thoroughly she had done her homework, but that she didn't press on about sensitive topics such as his parents splitting up and the fact that he hadn't wanted to live with his mother and her then boyfriend but had asked his aunt if he could stay with her for a while. Something that had been quite traumatic for a teenage boy to go through and had shaped him a lot. He had talked about it in his book, but never really got to the emotional bottom of it.

After a while he started to relax, and she noticed the shift. The groundwork had been laid. Every quote from now on was a bonus, she felt. Even if she didn't get anything out of him from now on, she had enough already to write a decent and interesting article. She didn't scribble down everything anymore, looked at him longer during his answers and leaned back in her chair. She had always liked him and his work. It took her by surprise how beautiful and appealing she found him, now that she had met him in person. So intelligent. So witty. So friendly, polite and gentleman-like. Sexy even. She had never thought of him in those terms. Also - he smelled wonderful, she had noticed when he shook her hand as they said hello in the narrow hallway. The aftershave was faint and his breath was pleasant.

"Stop it."

She was quite embarrassed to realise that she started to develop a bit of a crush the more she listened to him and the more she watched him. Not the most professional way to go about this endeavour. Especially as it was only to be the first of many meetings that were supposed to lead to an unbiased but insightful article. She tried to compose herself and ignore that she had started to like being in his company.

He is married. He is married. He is married.

As he finished an anecdote about the early years of his career, she started to scan her notes and suddenly stopped at one question that she was quite proud of, but hadn't intended to actually ask. No-one had asked this before. And she suddenly wanted to show him, that she understood his background. His story. His life. That she had a special insight. She wanted to impress him. It wasn't a question she would normally put this way. She would normally ask around it and hope that her interview partner would somehow be led to answer without her having to ask the question directly.

"You write in your book, that your wife, then girlfriend, was the first person you admitted to, that you wanted to become a comedian", she started now trying to sound very professional and inquisitive.

"Yes..."

"You were quite surprised that she didn't laugh in your face or think that this was the most ridiculous idea in the world. That in fact her reaction was as you would have expected some-one to react, if you told them about a very conventional car-eer-choice such as teacher, banker or accountant. Do you think that you would have become a comedian if she had reacted differently? Would you have chosen a different career, if she had deemed your dream job a ridiculous dream?"

Adam paused for a while. He was clearly taken by surprise. Emma regretted the question immediately. As proud as she had been, she suddenly realised what it implied. She had basically asked him not only what he would have chosen – his wife or comedy. She was also suggesting that his confidence as a com-edian, his idea of self-worth might just be hanging by the feeble thread that was his wife's goodwill, consent and support. If he was willing to give an answer, this could end up being the cen-tral hypothesis of the article... analysing the person behind the comedian.

He tried to smile at her.

"Ehmmm... I have never thought about it that way...", he tried to offer.

"Oh – by the way... do you want another cup of coffee?", he got up and grabbed her empty cup gesturing in the kitchen's direction.

"That would be lovely", Emma said and smiled. She got up as well and they walked over to the small kitchen to make some fresh coffee.

Emma decided to leave her question and direct the interview in a different direction as soon as they sat down again.

"A better journalist would now jump at this", she fretted. It was clear that she had hit an interesting point. Her journalistic instinct told her that this could be gold. She should just dig. But the journalist in her seldomly won.

"That is why I will always write the fluff pieces. The tame portraits", she thought.

But she didn't want to be too inquisitive. Investigative even. Leave that to other, more hungry, or maybe less scrupulous people. She felt people had the right to privacy. To things unsaid. She even believed in the government's right and even duty to secrets. To things being more complex than the news could reflect. She was very much in two minds about organisations such as Wikileaks. On the one hand, some things should be exposed, in the hope of changing them. Making the world a better place. Ideally. One tiny aspect at a time. Exposing wrong-doing for what it was. On the other hand... well... that was tricky. Sometimes, Emma was convinced, something so obviously wrong or immoral was necessary to make the world a better place. Make people safe. The greater good. The question was – who was to decide. She had no answer to that.

"I am in the wrong job", she sighed quietly pressed down with a lot of self-doubt as usual. She looked at Adam, hoping he wouldn't notice.

EMMA

The atmosphere in the green room was very relaxed, when Emma arrived. The guests were sitting together laughing, chatting, inspecting their goody bags with scented soaps and cheese, which were bizarre showbiz-gifts. Adam was listening to the host Bob talking about an especially horrible children's birthday he had recently been to with his three-year-old son. They were in stitches slagging off the weird new competitive tradition of throwing huge parties for little ones. Bouncy castles, clowns, magicians, weird novelty cakes and a guest list as long as those for weddings.

When Emma was ushered into the green room, Adam gave her a big smile and signalled to her, that he would be with her in a minute. He let Bob finish his anecdote. Then he excused himself and walked over to say hello.

She had missed him. It had been two weeks. The local run of his show was finished. He was now doing a television show and then he was supposed to take his show on the road.

He and Emma had sent a few e-mails back and forth about the arrangements in the up-coming weeks. She was very nervous about it, since they were supposed to go on the road together. He had three gigs. Three different cities. Her editor had suggested she should tag along. This wasn't a regular tour. Just three separate gigs, that his agent had convinced him to do for small charity organisations. Since they were so close together geographically and timewise, he had agree to do it.

And then in five weeks time from now there was the big summer party at his agency, which represented not only a lot of the most prominent comedians on the circuit, but also quite a number of successful actors. She would come along and watch him interact with his peers and other celebrities. Emma was nervous about the party. She didn't mind that much, that she would be in the same room with people she only knew from television and the cinema. Or that she had no idea what to wear and how to get ready to look all styled up. Although this was nerve-wrecking in itself. But she didn't know what her editor expected her to get from this. She thought it was ludicrous to think she would get anything genuine from watching him there, that she would be comfortable publishing. She had been trained to stick to the rule that you only publish something that either someone had said in a public context, such as a speech or a political debate, or agreed to be quoted. It would not be possible to stand next to Adam, listening, taking notes and constantly asking people whether or not she would be able to use whatever they had just said. They would not behave naturally anymore. And she would be a bloody nuisance. So far, she was planning to just let the photographer, who always turned up briefly at her meetings with Adam, get a few snapshots.

"Hi", Adam said. "How have you been?"

"Great. Thanks", she smiled at him, grateful, that he didn't let her wait in the corner. "And you?"

"Busy", he laughed. "The run is done."

"Adam..." Penny, a tall and sweet comedian, walked over and tapped Adam on his shoulder.

"Oh, sorry", she said and then laughed. "I didn't mean to interrupt. Oh, but hello, you must be Emma... Adam has told me all about you. If you need any stories about him... I am your girl", Penny said and smiled encouragingly.

"Funny, you should say that", Emma jumped immediately at the suggestion.

"For once my journalistic instincts are working", she thought, pleased with herself and excited to get a chance to talk to Penny. She had secretly hoped to not only meet her, as she was incredibly funny, but also to pick her brains about Adam, since they had worked together quite a bit in the past on various projects.

"Would you mind... can I quickly do an interview with you? Just a few minutes..."

"Sure", Penny was delighted. She took Emma by the arm and immediately dragged her over to a sofa in the corner.

BEN

"Cut it." Ben is pacing up and down behind me.

"Why?"

"It is boring. Irrelevant." He has become more and more impatient with me.

"Man, you are Mr. Charming today."

Ben stops.

"Why did you write this?"

"Penny, I guess. I wanted to introduce Penny."

"Do it later. You don't need her yet."

"But..."

"Come on... you can do better than this."

"Hey!" I am a little louder than I intended. "You can go and fuck right off!"

I slam the laptop shut and get up. I need some fresh air. I haven't kept to my schedule. I need to keep to my schedule. I have been caught up in writing too much. I need some normalcy. My fridge is empty. Shopping. I can hear Ben pacing upstairs. I grab my coat and a bag and walk out of the house.

The weather is warm, not too hot. A slight breeze. Perfect. I need to breathe. Long walk. The field. The brook. The woods. Just get out of the house. Away from those words. Away. Away.

There are a couple of dog walkers. I even meet two girls on horseback and a mother with two young children enjoying the sun, looking for field flowers and butterflies. Breathe. Breathe. Breathe.

On my way back I go by the shop to get some packed bread, biscuits, butter, cheese, pasta, a few vegetables and apples. Two bottles of orange juice and milk. I overdo it a little. The bag is heavy. I need to do my shopping on a more regular basis, I decide. Good intentions. Best laid plans of mice and men. My bloody schedules.

At home I put my shopping in the kitchen and walk into the garden. I don't even stop to listen for Ben. Check whether he is still pacing.

Nature has taken over once again. The lawn looks like it is trying to pose as the Pampa with long high blades of grass.

I start to rip out weeds in the flower and vegetable beds.

After two hours of ferociously working ripping and digging, I am dirty and sweaty. But the beds are starting to take some recognisable shape.

"Hello." A shy voice from the other side of the fence. I am startled.

"Hello...", I reply and look up. It is the neighbour's boy. He looks very uncomfortable, but tries to smile at me.

"Can I help you", I ask him.

"I wanted to ask you, if I could ... well, maybe, if you want... help to mow your lawn."

"For a bit of money, I assume."

He stares at his hands.

I am annoyed with myself. Clearly, his mother has put him up to this. There is no need to be rude to him. Embarrass him. I am such a cow sometimes. When did I become so unsociable? I sigh.

"It is very kind of you to offer", I even manage a smile. My back aches. I don't feel like pushing the lawn mower anytime soon.

"I could do with a little bit of help to be honest."

He looks up and smiles at me.

"Are you free right away? No need to wait till the weather gets bad again, right?"

He nods and I motion for him to climb over the fence which is ridiculously low anyway. Two hours later, he has improved his pocket money a little and my garden looks like one again. I put some lemonade on the porch and invite him to join me for a little break. I also put out some of the biscuits I bought earlier on.

"Thank you so much! I am glad you offered to help today. I don't think I would have been able to work my way through that wilderness", I tell him.

"Why do you let it grow so high", he asks me, immediately looking like he regrets the question. I get the distinct feeling, he is a little afraid of me.

"I haven't really noticed to be honest", I say truthfully. "I don't pay enough attention to my garden, I guess. It's a shame. I should really do more. It is such a nice garden."

I am surprised at myself. I feel quite comfortable around this boy. He must be about eleven or twelve years old. Still somewhat a child. He looks at me, genuinely listening. That hasn't happened to me in a long time. Ben listens. But that is not the same.

"So why aren't you paying any attention? What do you do?"

"I write."

"Cool!"

He seems so impressed, it makes me giggle a bit.

"What do you write?"

"Stories... nothing too specific... I am still trying to figure out, what I really want to write about. It was easier, when I was still working for the newspaper, you know. They tell you what to write about there."

"You could write about a superhero", he suggests. "Or a cowboy. Or a scientist making wonderful discoveries. An explorer – having adventures... ", he gets excited at all the ideas that seem to just flood his brain.

"Oh, I see there is a story-teller in you", I say. "Maybe I can pick your brain for ideas some time."

He nods and gives me a huge smile.

I suddenly have an idea.

"Tell me... how is you pocket money situation?"

"It's okay, I guess. But I am saving up for a telescope. I want to have a look at the stars and the moon and all that... it is taking a long time..."

"I have a proposal... As you have noticed, I am not very good at keeping my garden in shape and am in desperate need of some help. How about... you try to keep an eye on the state of my garden and help me a little keeping the grass cut and the weeds at bay... and in return I help you get your telescope a little earlier. You should probably ask your mum first, if she is okay with it. You being my employed gardener and all. I don't want to do this behind her back. And who knows... maybe we can come up with an explorer story along the way.

He doesn't have to answer really. His bright eyes and the big smile on his face are enough.

"It's a deal then..." I stretch out my hand and we shake on it.

"Wait... I don't even know your name", I suddenly realise as he walks over to the fence to get back home.

"I am Lucas", he says.

"I am very pleased, you climbed over my fence, Lucas. I am Anna."

It is getting dark, when I get upstairs. I have made tea and a sandwich.

Ben is sitting in his chair. He looks miserable.

I sit down and look at him.

"Never mind...", this is supposed to comfort him. But he refuses to look at me.

I put down the tea and the plate with the sandwich, get up and walk over to him. I kneel down in front of him and put my hands on his legs.

"I am sorry", he says.

"Don't be... I will cut it. Fuck it. No need to worry. You are right. It wasn't good. I have to find another way."

"You are in a better mood", he finally looks at me.

"I had a good day", I say and kiss him. I did not intend to. But I linger. Then I let my hands slowly run up his chest and put them around his neck. Then I pull him closer and kiss him again.

A little more passionate. I am a little surprised. He is kissing me back.

EMMA

"I don't believe this", Adam was getting really upset. He slammed the car door shut. "Two more on the list", he said and looked at her. Emma shrugged her shoulders and didn't say anything.

Someone had fucked up. It didn't really matter anymore, whether Adam's manager had made a mistake or the hotel had lost their reservation. One way or the other, they didn't have beds to sleep in.

They had arrived in the town at 4 pm. Enough time to check into the hotel. Get changed. Get some food. Emma knew a really nice curry house close to their hotel, as she had lived there for a while. Go to the venue and get ready for the gig. Really easy and relaxed.

The drive up had been a lot of fun. They had been laughing a lot. She had not taken any notes. Whatever was said, was private. She just wanted to get to know him. Not as a subject of her research. Just as a person.

When they arrived at the hotel they were in an almost giddy mood. But then, the young woman at the reception couldn't find their reservation.

"This must be a mistake", Adam said. "My manager booked those two rooms weeks ago."

"I am very, very sorry, sir", the woman got really uncomfortable. "It's not here."

"Well, can you get us something else?

"I am very, very sorry, sir", the woman said again. "We are completely booked out."

"Okay...", Adam stayed very calm and polite. There was still enough time to find something else. "Well, can you recommend another hotel close by?"

"You could try The Marriott just down the road", she suggested.

He thanked her. They left. At this point they thought it was pretty funny, that the reservation was lost. He was a little embarrassed. But still, mistakes happen.

They didn't have any luck at The Marriott. Or any of the next ten hotels. Even though they started to widen the perimeter of their search. Apparently there were a couple of events scheduled that weekend. Plus a bank holiday on Monday. They started to ask around at B&Bs. At 7 pm they still didn't have anywhere to stay. Adam started to get really nervous. The gig started at 8.

"Are you hungry?", he asked Emma, who for the last 15 minutes had just been walking next to him, not saying anything. The hilarity of the situation had worn off after they were rejected at every place, where they enquired.

"Yes, very", she said. "But that's okay... Let's just get a sandwich or a take-away or something and get to the theatre. You have to get ready. I am sure, they are already waiting for you."

They stopped at an Indian take-away and ordered. Emma waited for the food, while Adam ran over to the theatre. They would have to eat in the dressing room, while he was getting into his stage clothes. They would have to continue looking for a place to stay for the night after the show.

The director of the theatre couldn't really help either. Every hotel he suggested had already been checked off their list. He couldn't put them up in his house either he said, as his in-laws had come over for a visit. But he told his assistant to phone around and try to find a place for them to stay. Nothing came up. But there were five B&Bs on her list left, that she hadn't been able to call. They would try their luck there after the show.

The first two turned them down immediately. In the third the manager tried to make a few phone-calls to friends, but without any success.

There were only two more places left, when they got back into the car.

"I don't believe it", he said again. When he looked over at Emma again, he noticed how tired she looked. Not only had they been running around for hours, but she had also had a couple of long days of hard work and not a lot of sleep.

Once again, he started to contemplate their options. If they didn't get a room in one of the next two establishments, they would have no choice but to drive back home. Maybe look for a service station on the motorway with a motel. Or they could sleep in the car. He was also quite tired. So driving back wasn't exactly the most inviting option. But the night was quite chilly. Despite it being spring. So sleeping in the car wasn't great either.

They drove a couple of minutes before they reached the B&B called "Primrose Towers".

"Do you want to come in with me?", he asked as he saw some encouraging light in the downstairs windows.

"Sure", she said.

A grey-haired man in his sixties opened the door and let them in. He also didn't have any rooms available left. But Adam couldn't hide his disappointment anymore. So far, he had been very polite and calm every time they were turned away.

Then – as a joke – he said: "What about a couple of blankets? A couch? Sleeping bags? Anything? We'll sleep in the breakfast room on the floor, if you let us."

The old man gave him a surprised look.

"That desperate, eh?", he said. Then he paused to think. "I tell you what. My daughter moved out a few years ago. We still keep her room for when she visits", he started, still a little doubtful whether he should make the suggestion to let them stay there.

"It is a very plain and very small room. Just a bed and a cupboard. She took everything else with her, obviously. They grow up so fast, don't they. One minute a baby, the next, ... oh well. But it has its own little bathroom. We have our own quarters under the roof."

Adam wanted to hug the man. He had already started to wonder whether or not there would be an all-night supermarket anywhere to maybe buy blankets for a night in the car. And a customer toilet, where they could brush their teeth.

Even though Emma was very grateful for the offer, she realised that the man had said, a bed. Not two. One. They would have to share. The man assumed, that they were a couple.

The B&B-owner lead them up the stairs once they had got their bags out of Adam's car. On the third floor at the end of a very narrow corridor was the door to his daughter's room. He hadn't exaggerated. It was very small. The bed was big enough for two though. Not a double bed, but also not a simple single one either.

They said a thousand times thank you and then goodnight. Then they stood in the little room alone. Both dreadfully tired.

"I will sleep on the floor", Adam said, as he suddenly became aware of the situation. He had not thought about it. He had just been thankful that he didn't have to expose Emma to a cold night in the car. Now he became painfully aware of the one bed.

But before he could get any further with this, Emma said so firmly that it was clear she did not want to discuss this any further. "Non-sense. The bed is big enough for two. So let's just get changed and get some sleep." It sounded a bit harsh and matter-of-fact. More so than she had intended. She was actually very nervous about the prospect of sleeping next to him. To be physically this close. Nothing would happen between them. That was clear to her. Even though she wanted him badly. The man, she had to write about. The married man. He was off-limits. Her feelings and desires had to be completely inconsequential. They were two adults, who had restraint.

So, they got ready and got into bed.

EMMA

Emma had been very pleased with the article. Even though she had collected far too much material. This is usually not a good thing as you lose sight of what you want the story to be about. But she had found her theme. Easily. And she had enough anecdotes, quotes from a couple of people, material from the shows and impressions from the days she had spent with Adam to support it. It was a perfectly interesting read with a smooth flow and funny moments. Even her editor was pleased and told her so. That rarely happened. It was one of the best pieces she had ever written.

Emma worked for the magazine as a regular free-lancer. She covered everything that came up. Everything her editor wanted her to write about. Interesting or boring. Lengthy or just snippets. She worked in the office and from home. Anything. He often referred her to the local newspaper branch of the publishers as they were sometimes short of staff. Also even though Emma was flexible in the stuff she wrote, it was usually hardly enough to be able to live off just the magazine stuff. The paper editor would send her to human interest appointments, to court, to festivals, concerts, theatre or certain groups that had invited the press to one of their meetings. Anything really that needed coverage, but wasn't hard news.

The story about Adam had been a luxury piece. Not only did it very rarely happen that someone would get this much access for just one article. Also the publisher rarely covered those kinds of costs and would pay the appropriate kind of money for this much time invested. Emma had been very lucky. Most of the regularly employed colleagues had been quite envious. But, none of them had been prepared to spend this much time with Adam. They had too much other stuff on their plates. So the editor had asked her. The magazine issue was due to be out in two days. It had been proof-read. She had seen the layout. It was beautiful. There were some great pictures of Adam, who had had a studio session with the photographer earlier that month. There were a couple of pictures from the show. And a small one from a party.

She missed Adam. It had been two weeks since she had last talked to him. Two weeks. She had no reason anymore to contact him. No excuse rather. She was to leave him alone. Those were the rules. It was always that way. Only this time she hated it.

She picked up the kettle and poured hot water into the cup, which she had filled with slices of fresh ginger and a spoonful of honey. So far she hadn't minded living on her own. Being single for so long. She actually had enjoyed the freedom. You can do silly things without being judged. Pick your nose, scratch your bum, make ridiculous noises or refuse to brush your hair on a day in or fart loudly while sticking out your arse. But now, she felt lonely. For the first time in years it wasn't just a fancy she had taken to someone. She wanted to be with Adam. She took the steaming cup in both hands and walked over to her desk.

She hadn't heard from him since after that party. Obviously. He had taken her home in a cab. He had walked her to her door. "You look beautiful", he had said. Then he had leaned in and kissed her on the cheek. The kiss had taken a little longer than a gesture like that usually would. It was goodbye. They were both aware of it. But neither wanted to say it. So he kissed her a little longer instead. Then he said 'goodnight' and left.

She stared at her computer screen. A new assignment. City hall had bought a few sculptures by a local artist for the back garden of the main building. He was a boring arrogant prick. Not especially talented either. But it needed coverage. Yet she wasn't able to write even one word. She closed her eyes. For the

millionth time she thought of that kiss. His breath, his aftershave, the warmth of his skin.

EMMA

Court, always court. This was the fifth court case the newspaper had asked Emma to cover this week. And it was only Wednesday. Each time it was just a couple of lines she was required to write. The next case was three hours away. So she had sat down in the press room of the courthouse to write the short article there and send it to the editor, instead of going into the office. After that she wanted to get some lunch maybe, browse the book store across the street, get a coffee and sit in the sun for a while, before the next boring case was brought up before the judges. If only any of them had been interesting. Anything would do. But this was just thefts, illegal possession of weapons, and a case of credit card fraud. Nothing promised any exciting trips into the shady world of criminal masterminds. One young man got repeatedly caught stealing cigarettes at a corner store. One thought guns were cool, but was too stupid to get a license. He kept posing with the weapon in his garden till the neighbours got worried and reported him. And a middle aged woman found a credit card in a park. Instead of handing it over to the bank or the police, she had gone on a shopping spree on the internet for a bit. She didn't buy anything interesting or extravagant. Yes, they were big enough to be covered. But there was nothing weird or particularly interesting about them.

She walked down the stairs contemplating where to eat. There weren't a lot of good and inexpensive options in the area. She was so deep in thought, she almost walked into a man, as she turned the corner at the bottom of the stairs. Emma started to mumble "Sorry", when she looked up. Then she froze. It was

Adam.

"Hi", was all she could say. Then she noticed that Adam didn't look good. His eyes were a little red and puffy. He looked tired. He tried to smile.

"Hello…. ehmm… how are you?"

He didn't look too pleased to see her. Her heart sank.

"Fine, thank you." She almost didn't dare to ask him… "And… you?"

He gave a little sad laugh.

"Oh you know… peachy…", he said.

He had never been cynical or bitter before. She swallowed. And then she suddenly noticed the sign next to the big door, that said 'divorce court'. He followed her eyes and then shrugged his shoulders. He rubbed his eyes, trying to compose himself.

Then he said as firmly as he could manage: "Yep, I am not married anymore. Madelaine divorced me today."

Emma was confused. It had only been two months since the article had been published. They must have been separated already for a while even back then. Divorces usually took time.

"How long…?", she didn't know what else to say.

"Are you asking officially? Because… I am sorry, but I don't want this in the papers."

"Why didn't you tell me?", she whispered. She was hurt, that he had pretended to be happily married. And why did he feel the need to distrust her? Why did he assume she immediately wanted to write about it? Of course she knew the answers to all this. But it hurt her nevertheless.

He looked her in the eyes for a long time without saying anything. Then he looked at his feet.

"You know why", he finally said. "It was none of the magazine's business. I had no intention to tell anyone. Most of our friends didn't know for a long time. And then… I couldn't tell you anymore after a while…", he sighed, still struggling. "Fuck!", then he laughed frustrated. "I had more than a whole fucking year to get used to the thought, that this day would come. And still, there we were. And this judge just said a few words, we all sign a paper... and it is done. Over. For good." Then he started laughing again. "And then, of all the people in the world... you are the one to catch me in the corridor crying."

"I am not going to write about it", she said.

"That is not what I meant."

ANNA

"Divorcee it is then...", Ben did not look completely convinced. "Did you mention that he was married?"

"I don't know", I confess. "I changed it around so much." I pause. "Do you like the scene? The twist?"

"Twist? I didn't know that marriage was the obstacle. I thought, they were too stupid. Or too much wrapped up in their work ethic. Don't sleep with the object of your article or something of the kind."

"I should make this more clear, shouldn't I..."

"You think?"

I sigh.

"Never mind. Rewrite. Rewrite. Rewrite. My mantra, it seems to be."

Ben laughs.

"Yes... I like it", he says so suddenly that I feel the need to turn around to check if I have misheard him.

He smiles at me.

EMMA

"Why the hell are you so upset?" Lilly didn't understand the emotional uproar. "First you were upset, that he was married. Now you are upset, that he got divorced. Be happy. He is available."

"But he lied to me", Emma knew that was a very weak argument to make, as she understood why he had done so. It sounded very lame, when she said it. She knew that, Lilly knew that. That was very clear in the mocking look her best friend gave her. Also it wasn't quite true. He had never explicitly said, that his marriage was happy. Or mentioned his marriage for that matter. He had just never talked about it. So it was more a false assumption on her side, that he had failed to correct. Strictly speaking. Also, that wasn't the reason, why she was upset.

Emma shrugged and didn't say anything for a while. Staring at the mug in her hand. The tea was already getting cold.

Adam had left the courthouse, immediately after their short conversation. The situation hadn't really changed. They had no reason to see each other again. She would have no opportunity to take advantage of his divorced status. Also... you don't throw yourself at someone who had just gone through a divorce. He was almost as unattainable as before.

There was no point in arguing about this again with Lilly. Lilly had been the only person Emma had admitted her feelings for Adam to. Well, at least to some extent. She had felt obliged to tell her. Girlfriends do tell each other these things.

Lilly and Emma had grown up on the same street. And though Lilly was two years older, they became friends early on.

They had lived through every little and big disaster, every joy, every excitement, heart-break or trouble with the family. They were very different in their approach to life and love. But they loved each other.

When Emma told Lilly, she shrugged her feelings for Adam off as an infatuation. A crush. She was a little star-struck, but realistic and just needed someone to talk to, to get over it. Fast. She didn't tell her friend that Adam was always on her mind. That she was worried, that it was love and not just desire. Either way, Lilly didn't want to hear about the sitting still, and getting over the crush scheme. She didn't care about the unspoken sanctity of the short-lived journalist-subject arrangement. Emma admired her. Whenever Lilly had fallen in love, she had just gone for it. She got rejected and crushed, sometimes found romance or a flirt, twice even love. But she never regretted anything.

She told her again, to just call Adam and suggest a date.

How inappropriate, Emma thought. And to what end would that date go, if it actually happened, she wondered. Adam was hardly relationship material at the moment, she would guess. He had looked so shaken and saddened. She had wanted to comfort him, but didn't know how. So she had just stood there. Awkwardly. And then he had said goodbye.

What was worse than Adam being possibly an emotional wreck at the moment, was the notion, that he probably didn't feel the same about her. Yes, they had gotten on so well. She had felt the sparks. But what if she was mistaken? What if it was just her? If there hadn't been a special something between them? He was nice to everyone. What if she just imagined it all? So far it had been almost easy to just blame history. He had met Madelaine over twenty years before Emma crossed his path. He was already taken. In another time, another universe... It had consoled her as well as tortured her. Now she was scared. That she wouldn't have the courage to do anything about it. That it was the wrong time. That he was just indifferent.

The phone rang.

"Hello..."

"Hi, is that Emma? The journalist?"

"Yes..."

"Oh goody. This is Penny. Do you remember me? We met at the party. We talked about Adam for your article. Great article by the way. Really spot on. Nailed him on the head. Or something like that. But then, you had great interview partners, who made you see, right. Haha. Such as Moi."

"Eemmh... Hi...eemmh... Thank you..."

"Oh, in case you are wondering, I got your number through my agent from your editor. I hope this is alright."

"No...yes... of course... that is alright..."

"Who is it?", Lilly whispered while wildly gesturing.

Emma gestured back for her to shut up.

"What can I do for you?"

"Oh, eh..., well, I don't know if you are for hire... As a writer I mean. Not anything like a stripper or anything like that. Obviously. Haha. Well, we need someone to write something about the new season of my sitcom. Something we could offer the magazines. My agent just fired the person in his office who usually does that sort of stuff. Bad timing. We need something to send out urgently. Press release and stuff. And since I liked your article about Adam, I thought, maybe you would be interested in coming down to the set – maybe even today – and talking to the advertising people and writing something. I am not sure about the money... but if you are interested, come down to the studio and we'll talk, okay."

Penny just quickly gave her the address, her phone number to call, to let her know which decision Emma had made, and a time. Then she said goodbye and hung up, before Emma could contemplate the job – or anything she had said.

"Soooo... you look like you have seen a ghost...", Lilly was curious.

"That was Penny. The Penny Dermott. She wants me to write about her show."

"Cool! When?"

"Today... Now..."

"And?"

"I don't know... I guess, I'll go there and see what exactly they want. She wasn't very specific."

"Isn't she friends with Adam?", Lilly gave her a triumphant smile.

Emma was nervous. Adam wouldn't be there. He had nothing to do with Penny's show. But Penny was from his world. And Emma would re-enter that world. If only briefly.

EMMA

When Emma came to the studio, Penny talked a lot, made her an offer for the article, immediately suggested lunch together for the next day. They talked about a movie, they were both excited about and agreed to go and see it together.

Penny called her a couple of times. They met for coffee and lunch a few times. Emma came along on a Sunday walk with Penny and her dog. Then the comedian found a couple of other little writing jobs for Emma on the show. She proved to be very funny. So much so, that one of the producers was quick to offer her a permanent job on the writing team supporting Penny, who was the main creative force behind the scripts. After three weeks, Penny invited Emma to a weekend away with some of her friends. One of the girls, so Penny reasoned, had had to cancel at the last minute and so one of the rooms was vacant. They needed an extra person to come along. So? Would she fancy the trip? Emma said yes. They had become friends after all.

They – which was eight people all in all, including now Emma, all singles, no couples allowed - were staying at an old converted farmhouse in the countryside. Several bedrooms, a big communal kitchen, a wonderful yard, a pond, beautiful landscape and wonderful walks all around. Just an hour outside the city. Easily reached by train. The weather was wonderfully warm. A golden late summer.

Penny hadn't told Emma, which friends would be coming along. Emma hadn't asked. She had assumed, some friends outside of showbiz.

They arrived separately on the Friday evening. Emma offered to cook for everyone on the first night. An Iraqi dish calledfasoliawas her choice as it was her favourite. Lamb with beans, rice, tomatoes and bread. The wonderful thing about fasolia was the unique mix of spices. Lots of cinnamon and pepper. Apart from the bread that needed a little bit of preparation, and the chopping of the meat and tomatoes, the dish was very quickly and easily put together.

The food was already simmering in the big pan, when Emma noticed that she had left her phone upstairs in her room. Lilly had gone on a blind date that night. She usually wrote Emma a quick note, whether the evening looked promising or not. And she expected a quick note back. That was their routine. So Emma lowered the heat and went upstairs.

She found her phone quickly in her bag. No message yet. A good sign. Whenever a date went bad, Lilly excused herself quickly to the bathroom to complain about, why she never found any gorgeous guys on the dating website, or the office, or the park, or a café, or a party ...or anywhere else for that matter. When a date went really well... well, then there might not be a message till the next morning. But that was rare.

So far, Penny's friends all seemed to be nice. Not all of them had arrived yet. Two were still missing. They all offered to help in the kitchen. But there was just not enough to do and Emma enjoyed preparing a meal on her own for other people. At least then she could take all the credit – or blame.

Milly and Sarah had arrived together in the afternoon, just after Emma. Penny had already got there in the morning to get a few things sorted. Tom and Gary joined them only a little later. They were immediately all talking at the same time, catching up. They made a little small-talk with Emma, got to know her a little, asked what she did. Tom had read a few of her articles in the magazine and asked her about some of the stories.

Even though she felt a little uncomfortable as the newcomer in this group of long-time friends, she felt very welcome and was looking forward to a fun weekend.

Ironically it was helping to take her mind off Adam. Penny never mentioned him. At first, Emma had hoped she would. But then she was glad that Adam didn't feature in their conversations. This way, it would be easier to get over him. She was determined now to get over him. Emma had been convinced that it would be hard not to ask about him. To hide her feelings from her new friend. But she was doing well. Even Lilly had given up pestering her about it.

Emma slipped her phone in her pocket and opened the door to go back downstairs to take care of the food.

"Hi..."

She had almost crashed into Adam, who was just coming up the stairs.

"Hi."

For a moment they stood in silence, staring at each other.

"I didn't know, you were going to be here", Adam finally said.

"Penny asked me to come along. There was one spare room."

"Penny? I didn't know, you were in touch."

"Well...", Emma didn't know how explain her new friendship with Penny.

Adam suddenly smiled at her. "It's nice to see you ... - I just put my stuff in my room and see you downstairs, okay..."

"Okay." Emma was too dazed to say anything else. So she just went downstairs back into the kitchen. The stew was bubbling nicely. It was time to put the rolled out bread dough into the pan. 15 minutes later the food was done. Penny and Milly had already set the table. Emma was introduced to Alexandra, who had just walked in with two huge bags over her shoulders. Adam hadn't come down yet.

Then Emma just excused herself, without anyone taking too much notice, and locked herself in the bathroom. Her hands were shaking, her face was hot. She had never contemplated the possibility, that Adam would be one of the friends, Penny had invited for the weekend. It had never crossed her mind. And now he was here. All her effort to get over him was wiped away in one small moment. And they would have to spend the whole weekend together.

"Oh god... stop panicking... it's alright, it's alright... not to worry.... Shit..."

There was no real time to stay in the bathroom long enough to properly brace herself without raising suspicion. After all, they were about to eat her food. So she needed to be there. She breathed in deeply one more time, looked at herself in the mirror and then walked out.

The others loved the fasolia. Everyone was full of praise. For a moment she was the centre of attention. Happy munching, licking of lips, relaxed chatter, a lot of laughter... Emma started to relax a little bit. Adam smiled at her, but didn't say anything.

When she started to pick up the dishes to clear the table after they were all done and happily fed, everyone protested immediately.

"You stay where you are", Sarah commanded her. "You cooked, we'll clean up. Sit."

"Coffee, or tea anyone", Penny trilled. Everyone put in an order and off she went, while the others fussed with the dishes, still talking non-stop and all at the same time.

"Don't worry", Milly whispered amusedly in Emma's ear. "We are like an excited flock of birds just for the first couple of hours. Then we calm down a little bit. We don't see each other that often." She shrugged, laughed and gave Emma an encouraging nudge.

Adam wasn't one of this tight group of people. That became clear very quickly. Like Emma, he was a relative newcomer. He had met them all individually before. Even as a group. At Penny's house. For barbecues, a birthday party, as a friend who came along to a studio recording or to a lunch during rehearsal, when Penny was still working with Adam on one of his shows. But it was fair to say, that he wasn't close to any of them, except Penny herself.

They took the trip to this old farmhouse every year. It had become a tradition that had started when Penny had met Tom, Gary and Alexandra at university. Most of them were in relationships by now. Even married. But their partners were not allowed to come along. It was the first time that someone else outside of their group had been invited along. The reason was that Susan and Mike, the two missing people from their circle and also university friends, were both abroad this year. Susan had to attend a business meeting in the US and Mike had gone to his brother's wedding in France. Really bad timing. They could have easily split the cost of the two extra rooms, but Penny had convinced the others to ask two of her friends along. Why not? Just this time. Such fun. No objections were made by anyone.

The sun was about to set behind the hill. The air had already that chilly evening feeling about it. The only warmth came from the barbecue across the yard. Tom and Gary talked about some work related stuff, laughed and kept flipping the food. The girls sat at the table giggling and talking about some embarrassing thing that had happened to them some other weekend a couple of years ago. Emma wasn't really listen. She was sitting on a bench a little apart from the group watching the sunset. Taking in the last bit of warmth, before it turned into twilight. She closed her eyes. The day had been a lazy one. They had taken a long walk together around the lake and through the nearby woods. Milly had cooked a wonderful soup for lunch. Penny and Gary had gone to town to get some food for the barbecue. Apart from that, the day had been filled with chats, laughter, and sitting in the sun in the yard. Most of the time, they were all there. Emma just listened and enjoyed the company. Only very rarely did she get involved in one of their conversations. Adam also kept very much to himself. No-one seemed to notice that they were both very quiet. They were all too busy having fun, discussing films, T.V. shows, music, celebrity crushes, promotions, future plans, weddings they had been to, and old friends they had bumped into, who had gotten divorced, married, had bought an ugly house or had babies. Gossip ruled the day as much as repeated trips down their common memory lane, to which Emma and Adam had no access. So they kept to themselves. Each on their own.

She still had her eyes closed. The chatter had become white noise. She could hear the crickets and a few frogs. For a moment she felt a little at peace. She hadn't been able to sleep very well. Knowing Adam was in the room next to hers. Just a few feet between them. Both their rooms were on the upper floor. Just underneath the roof.

But so far she had been able to keep her calm. At least she was sure no-one had noticed what a turmoil ruled her thoughts. She wanted to hide. At the same time she wanted desperately to talk to Adam. She wanted to be near him. Laugh with him. Look into his eyes. Kiss him. Touch him. Be with him. She took a deep breath and then opened her eyes again and almost jumped.

"Hey", Adam was standing in front of her with two cups of tea in his hands. He held out one to her.

"Thank you", she said composing herself quickly again. Her heart had stood still for a second.

"Sorry, I didn't mean to startle you", Adam said. "Can I join you?"

"Sure", Emma moved a little bit to the side to make room for him.

They sat in silence for a moment. She held her cup in both hands. Glad to have something to hold on to, to focus her attention on.

When they both turned their heads and looked at each other for a moment they both smiled, not knowing what to say.

"It shouldn't be this hard, right", Adam suddenly said. Then he breathed in sharply and laughed. "Okay... here we go... How have you been?"

Emma was perplexed. "Ehm... Fine... Busy, I guess... And you?"

"Good... good... busy, too", he looked at her a little relieved.

"So you and Penny have become friends."

"Yes... I guess... She called me and invited me to do some work for her show. I am not exactly sure why she thought of me. She has been extremely nice to me."

"She is a wonderful person", Adam said. The girls at the table bust out in roaring laughter. "I really regret she left my show. But she is just too talented not to do her own thing. That is the risk of hiring the best. They just wander off on their own after a while."

"Those scenes with her are some of the best", Emma agreed and laughed.

"She is so funny, when she forgets her lines", now Adam was laughing. "She tends to swear a lot. Really dirty. You wouldn't believe."

"Oh, I do", Emma was so glad, they were talking again. Comfortable talking. But just as the nervousness slowly slipped away.

"Who wants steak?", Gary had turned around from the grill and waved some meat around. "The aubergines and the sausages are also done, I think", he said.

Emma and Adam hesitated a moment, then got up, picked up plates, some food and sat down with the others to eat. Even though they were back to not talking – for now – things had changed.

It felt like she hadn't really made a clear decision. She just acted. She grabbed everything that was lying around in the room and hastily stuffed it in her bag. Her pyjamas, the hairbrush, the toothpaste, the charger for her mobile phone, the novel, a t-shirt, the tissues. No time to pack properly. Everything just landed in the bag, carelessly stuffed in. When she stepped out of the room she heard arguing from downstairs. Adam was shouting. Penny was swearing back at him. A door was slammed. She didn't hear the rest as she rushed down the stairs, passed Milly in the hallway and pushed towards the front-door.

"Emma...", Milly half-heartedly tried to stop her.

It was dark outside. And cold by now. Emma didn't care. It was about one and a half miles to the train station. Maybe two. Less than 20 minutes if she hurried a bit, she reckoned. She threw her backpack over her shoulders and walked down the dark road. The last train to the city was in half an hour. She hoped that it would actually turn up. She didn't want to stay in the village a minute longer than necessary. Her face was burning, her breathing was rapid as she rushed along the road. She was usually afraid of the dark. But that didn't matter at that moment. Her mind was racing. She was not able to identify a clear thought. She wanted to get away. Get back to her flat.

It had been a very nice meal. Gary and Tom had used a lovely marinade with fresh herbs, spices, yoghurt and mustard to prepare the vegetables and some of the meat as well. While she only drank water and tea as she didn't like booze, and had learned to act accordingly, withstanding the pressure of social conventions, the others had started to open one wine bottle after the other. It got louder and louder, and gradually more and more foul-mouthed. She didn't mind. As long as no-one forced her to drink along. Adam was also not drinking.

Then Milly had suggested they'd play 'truth or dare'. Emma hated games. Especially that one. She hated the pressure not only of having to fulfil a dare, but especially to come up with something original to ask the others or challenge them with. But it started all fun and harmless and sparked some fun conversations and confessions as everyone chose 'truth' to begin with. Gary had cheated in his final exams in school, Penny had lied to her mom about spending the night at her best friend's, when really she went on her first date and Sarah had once stolen stationary from her office, but felt so guilty that she replaced everything the next day. Adam only holidayed close by as he was shit-scared of flying.

Emma's first truth-question was 'When did you loose your virginity?'. Milly had asked her. 24 had been her truthful answer.

"Wow, that is late", Milly was puzzled. "Why? You are not

exactly ugly..." Emma started to laugh.

"Thanks ... I guess ... it just didn't happened before. First I wasn't ready, and then when I was, no-one wanted to be the first one", she added with an mock-hurt laugh. "Anyway, when the next guy came along, I pretended to be a little more experienced than I was. And it happened on the first date."

Emma decided to be a little more honest about it than necessary, as she was enjoying being included in the group for the moment and feeling brave. She also didn't want Adam to think that she was some kind of prudish old bore.

"Three times in a row that night... walking was painful the next day."

"Oh, you dirty bitch", Gary shouted and the group howled with drunken laughter, while Emma smiled with a mixture of triumphant pleasure and embarrassed blush.

As the game carried on, the group got braver and the 'dares' became more and more frequent. At first they were silly and drink-oriented. There was not a lot they could do in the dark yard. Tom had to try and do a head-stand, and failed miserably, falling down laughing. Alexandra hated it to sing in front of other people and was promptly asked to serenade the nursery rhyme "Twinkle, twinkle, little star".

But then Penny had turned to Adam.

"Truth or dare?"

"Dare..." It was more an unsure question, than a statement. But Adam didn't seem to want to chicken out.

Penny smiled drunkenly, with triumph in her eyes. She had waited for this moment.

"I dare you...(dramatic pause) to kiss Emma and tell her how much you love her really."

Everyone fell quiet.

Penny started laughing and looked around.

"Come on, it is so obvious, that you are gagging for it. And she is too. So just slip her one."

Adam was staring at his shoes.

Then suddenly as if this had been on everybody's mind,

Penny added: "Oh, and don't worry, the beds are big enough and don't squeak too much, right Milly? You would know, wouldn't you? Ended up in one of them with Gary one year, didn't you? Hahaha."

"Will you please stop talking now", Milly put her hand on Penny's arm, but she pushed her away.

"No, no, Milly, those two fancy each other like mad and should do it. Right here, right now. Come on, it's shag time. Well, kiss... but you know what that will lead to. Nudge-nudge, wink-wink. You know, that is why I invited them along. Remember? We talked about it. He hasn't had sex in over two and a half years now, you know. Embarrassing. Probably won't last very long, I guess, poor girl", she said behind her hand and started to laugh again.

It was supposed to be a whisper to Milly. But Penny had no control over her speaking volume anymore. Then she suddenly remembered the game and almost bounced up on the couch, enthusiastically clapping her hands together.

"Oh, yes, right, goody. Such fun! Go on, Adam, I dare you." Then just as out of the blue, Penny got up, almost stumbling over and announced somewhat theatrically swinging her arms around, which started to challenge her balance in a quite menacing manner: "Whoops, coming through, I better get some rubber johnnys. You can't be too careful these days. I don't think she's had any sex either for a long while... but then I don't know Emma too well and you never know where she has been, right. Also no preggers, please."

Then she clumsily left the room muttering to herself and giggling.

In the uncomfortable silence that followed, Emma didn't want to wait for Penny to get back with the condoms. So she got up and rushed out without looking at anybody.

She could already see the lights of the train station. She slowed down a little bit. There was still enough time before the train arrived.

Adam had said nothing. He had just sat there, staring at his feet. When the shouting started, she had already been upstairs packing. She had no idea, what Adam had said to Penny.

She arrived at the train station. Everyone who had gone into the city for a night of clubbing or theatre or whatever the metropolis had to offer over the country had taken a ride hours ago. This was the last one for the night. The next one wouldn't pull into the station till five o'clock in the morning. She had checked the schedule on her mobile on her walk to the station. She sat down on a dodgy looking bench, just because it was the closest to the only light illuminating a small part of the platform. The village had a very small stop. Commuters only. If you wanted to go anywhere you first had to get into the city. But at least the trains ran regularly every hour till quite late.

She felt numb. Her head hurt. She tried to concentrate on her breathing rather than think about anything. She didn't want to have a puffy cried-out face on her, when she got on the train with its harsh light. No pitying looks, please. So she pushed every thought aside about Adam, about Penny. It had to wait till she got home. She took three very calm breaths.

It was almost midnight. Five more minutes till the train was due.

A car pulled up next to the train station. When she looked over she knew immediately that it was Adam. He got out and rushed over. He looked shaken. He sat down next to her and didn't say anything at first.

"Are you going home?", he finally asked.

"Yes..."

He nodded his head.

"Me too."

She looked over to his car. His bag was on the back-seat.

Without looking at her, he pleaded: "Please, let me give you a lift home. Please don't take the train."

She didn't say anything. This time it was her, starring at her feet. Not knowing what to do.

"I haven't been drinking... if you are worried...", he suddenly added. "But I guess you already know that."

The train pulled in. When it came to a stop she got up and picked up her bag.

"Please...", Adam repeated.

For a moment she didn't move. Then she started walking towards his car, while the train started pulling out of the station again.

The whole drive back into the city they sat in silence. It took them a little longer than usually as there had been a car crash. Emma stared out of the window to avoid any eye contact. She fought the tears back. She was sure that if she allowed herself to acknowledge Adam's presence only inches away from her, if she allowed herself to engage with him in any way she wouldn't be able to hold up anymore. So she kept staring. The other cars, the lights of the city, it all flew by. Nothing registered. Then Adam slowed down. She realised that they were already in front of her building. She had dreaded the moment Adam would have to ask her directions. But he had remembered. She looked at him in surprise. All those months. And he remembered. He had given her a lift home once. After the party.

He turned off the engine and got out of the car to get her bag out of the trunk.

Now she had to face him. Talk to him. At least thank him for driving her home. Something. She couldn't just walk off. She realised that this could be the last time she saw him. The last few moments. She had not thought about what to do now. He held the door open for her. She was annoyed with herself. She should have got out before. Shown some initiative maybe. It was too late. So she climbed out of the car.

They started to walk to her front-door together. He was still carrying her bag. Emma tried desperately to come up with some strategy to save the moment. To do something that would save whatever it was that had been there between them. Whether or not it was just in her head. She needed to untarnish it again. To cleanse it from the bitter after-taste of this strange evening. But then far too quickly they were standing in front of her door. She turned around, still unable to look at him.

"I am sorry", Adam said.

Her stomach cramped. The silence was broken. She had been unable to end this on her terms. Whatever those were.

"I am so sorry, that I never called you."

What was he talking about? Emma finally looked up. He looked upset. Nervous.

"I thought about it so many times... I just...", Adam was struggling. He looked determined. Like he had thought about what to say to her. Like he had a plan and had worked up the nerve to set it in motion. Tell her, whatever it was, he needed to say. It had never occurred to her, that he might have something to say as well.

"Penny is right you know... It wasn't her place to say anything...", he laughed bitterly, shaking his head. "But you know... she is right."

He looked up. Directly into her eyes.

"I ..." He swallowed. Then he took a step towards her and kissed her. Very carefully.

Her fingertips tingled. She couldn't breathe for a moment. Her whole body melted under his touch. She opened her lips slightly and pushed herself against him. Her hands first on his chest, then around his neck. She needed to hold onto him, not to fall. She lightly pressed her lips against his. Feeling his warm breath. His skin. When they broke apart and looked at each other, he gently touched her cheek. She felt tears running down her face. For so long she had held them in. He wiped them away, kissed her cheeks. Then she kissed him again. A little more forcefully. She had wanted him for so long. And here he was now in her arms. His warm body. He smelled so wonderful. She would not let him go again. Then she turned around, took out her key, unlocked and opened the door and took Adam's hand.

"Rise and shine", Milly had a cup of hot steaming coffee in her hand as she noisily sat down on the chair next to the couch. She put the cup in front of her friend. Penny tried to lift her head, but immediately gave up the effort as it felt like a huge block of lead was attached to it, holding it down.

"What the fuck...", she moaned. "Why am I on the couch and not in my bed?"

"Oh... you don't remember?", Milly looked pissed off, which worried Penny. Her friend was never angry with her. Well, never say never. Once Penny had put quite a strain on their friendship by embarrassing Milly in front of the guy she had been terribly infatuated with for months. But that was at school. In another lifetime.

"What happened?", Penny decided to force herself to sit up, holding her head as she was sure, it would snap right off. "Ouch..."

"Sore head, have we?", Gary came in. He was also not exactly pleased with her. What was wrong with everybody this morning?, Penny wondered. Yes, she had had more to drink than usual. But that was no reason to get all pissy and judgy. They had all been hammered as well, as far as she could recall. It had been such fun. Hmm... such fun. When Sarah, Tom and Alexandra walked in and passed her on their way to the dinner-table to prepare breakfast without so much as a "good morning", Penny started to get annoyed.

"What the fuck is going on?", she cringed and rubbed her temples as the outburst had been far too loud for her sore head.

"Well thank your lucky stars and the fact, that we generally all love you, that no-one is beating you with a stick shouting abuse at you right now", Tom said without even bothering to look over.

"Why? I am sure, that whatever I have done – I can't remember anything, thank you very much, - can't be so bad, that you are all being such meanies." Penny started to feel unfairly treated and really sorry for herself.

"Where are Adam and Emma?", Penny suddenly noticed the absence of the two additions to their usual party. At the mention of their names, not only did the others give each other meaningful worried looks, it also jump-started some part of her memory. Penny froze in realisation.

"Oh god…", then she buried her face in her hands.

"Yupp… here it is, she remembers", Milly got up from the seat and walked over to the dinner-table.

Adam was red in the face, as he shouted at her.

"What the fuck, Penny! Who do you think you are, you mad cow?"

"Calm down, mate…"

Penny never said "mate".

"You know you want her."

"That is none of your business! And anyway… we would have been fine sorting it out on our own! None of what you call 'help' needed. Thanks very much. But there won't be a chance of it happening now, will there."

"Aha! It! There is an 'It' to be sorted out! Told you!"

Penny felt great. She was such a good match-maker. Right on the money. They would include her in their speeches at the wedding. She could already see herself modestly, but proudly – and obviously dressed in a beautiful gown - receiving all those touching looks from all the wedding guests, as Adam told them the heart-warming story of how Penny, and Penny alone, had been responsible for their ever-lasting, passionate love. Oh thank you, no, really, it was nothing. What are friends for after all.

"Hey – snap out of it", Adam was really angry. "What the fuck were you thinking."

"Oh fuck off, you repressed idiot. You should be grateful somebody is actually taking an interest in your love-life, dear. Well, non-existent one, right now, if we are honest. I am being really kind to revive it, don't you think!"

"It is not your job to revive it! That's the point! And now you've probably just killed whatever was left…"

"Go on, tell her, give her a good snog and then boom-chic-kee-bow-wow… shaggy-dee-doo…", Penny formed a circle with her left thumb and index finger and pushed her right index-finger through it, back and forth. "Oh yes, Adam, give it to me, ooohhhh, aahh...."

"Fuck off. There is no point talking to you, right now. I am leaving", Adam slammed the door as he stormed out of the room.

"Drama queen...", Penny had laughed. How amusing he was. So lovable. Cute cuddly teddy bear.

"Oh please, please, please, tell me I didn't do that", Penny wasn't able to look up, she was so ashamed. She was still hiding behind her hands. Then she suddenly jumped up, despite the piercing pain that shot through her head, caused by the fast movement and ran to the bathroom to throw up.

Those green-blue eyes with the most beautiful crows' feet. The two little dimples on each side of his mouth, when he smiled or laughed. Emma couldn't get enough of looking at Adam. It felt surreal. Him in her bed. Like he would be gone if she dared to let him out of her sight. Just disappear. Like a dream. She needed to touch him all the time, just to make sure she wasn't imagining him being there. The muscles in her face were sore. Smiling, laughing. She couldn't stop. The kissing. Her lips felt raw. Her chin was red from his stubbles.

She let her fingertips run over his chest.

"How come you had those three condoms in your wallet?"

He started to laugh.

"Oh god, I was afraid you would finally ask that, once you came to your senses again." He looked at her. "Promise you won't laugh... or think less of me?"

"Hmmm... dangerous promise to make... no... can't do... tell me nevertheless?"

"Well, it's one of the very few pieces of advice I took from my dad after he left us. He told me I should always have three condoms on me at all times."

Adam looked a little embarrassed.

"Always ready for responsible action so to speak", Adam chuckled and shook his head. "I was only twelve. It sort of stuck. I always have three condoms on me. It became like a superstitious thing. Not the same ones obviously as they would be out of date and unusable at some point. It is something I check before I leave the house, like 'Do I have my keys and wallet' or 'Have I switched off the oven'. It's a little bit of an obsession", Adam shrugged his shoulders and added: "He didn't give me a lot of manly advice."

"It's an odd bit of advice."

"He hated the idea of missed opportunities."

"So you always had three condoms on you since the age of twelve?"

"Yes."

Adam started to hide behind his hands.

"Even during your marriage?"

"Ehmmm... yes..." Then he looked at her, now a little worried that she might get the wrong idea.

"I hardly ever got to use any of them. You wouldn't believe how many condoms I had to throw away because they were out of date... Madelaine knew about this by the way. She found it weird, but I think she knew that they were never intended to cheat on her. They were just... I don't know... a safety net. I know, it's silly. It just became habit. My father was very forceful giving out this advice. As if I would immediately die of syphilis or father hundreds of babies, if I didn't carry them, even if I never touched a woman in my whole life. It was all about the condoms in my pocket. He never told me to use them, now come to think of it. And for years I didn't think they would be put into use at some point... I was a bit of a late bloomer. The penny didn't drop till I was about seventeen. And then it took me another two years to find someone who was willing to set that new found knowledge into action."

"Did he say why it had to be three exactly?"

Adam thought about it a moment.

"No... Maybe because three is a magic number? Or I guess,

because it is unlikely that between spontaneously jumping into bed and being able to buy some new ones, you will be able to get it up more often than three times at the most. To assume anything else would be bragging", he now grinned, pushing his hand up her inner thigh, kissing her and rolling on top of her, he reached for the box of condoms on the bedside table that Emma had taken out of her cupboard earlier on. Leftovers from her previous relationship. They had to use them up, she had announced. The expiry date was coming up.

The Sunday of five times, their first weekend, would certainly stay in their memory.

Her phone made a noise again.

"Don't you want to answer her? Put her out of her misery?", Adam started to laugh. "It's kind of hard to be mad at her now, isn't it."

"Hmmm...", despite the many hours in bed and it being already Monday morning, Emma didn't want to move. She just wanted to stay put. Cuddled up in bed. Catching her breath. Letting the sweat dry. The memory of him inside her, was still very fresh. Emma was happy that there were no appointments, no work, nothing that they had to get up for. But of course he was right. She was far too happy to be mad at Penny, who had left numerous messages. Apologising over and over again. Trying to explain. Trying to play down everything. She sounded miserable, though desperately trying to be chirpy.

"Should we tell her?", Adam suddenly asked. "Or... should we just accept the apology for now and keep this our secret?"

"What do you want to do?"

"Stand on top of the world and shout out, how happy I am." He rolled over, laughed and kissed her again playfully.

"Right... call her. Tell her."

He grinned and jumped out the bed.

"Do you feel like going out for breakfast?", he asked grabbing his phone.

SATURDAY

One paw in front of the other. Again and again. One paw in front of the other. The cat never breaks its pace. Round after round. Over the tree trunk, along the little clear pool, across the small trodden path through the leaves, around under the net, disappearing for a bit out of sight behind the rock and back on the tree trunk. The habitat is beautifully designed. A lot of thick plants to stand in for the vastness of the rainforest.

I can hear birds. The squeaking sound of the tapirs that seem to be in mating season. The impatient screams of the giant otters. It is almost time for their food. At least that is what it said on the little sign earlier on next to their luxuriant habitat with the beautiful big pool, the little stream running down the side of the enclosure. All those tall trees with wildly jumping white-faced sakis.

The fishing cat that keeps pacing past that big window along the pool is from Asia.

"Did you know, that this cat has webbing? The little fucker actually enjoys swimming!" Rachel is almost shouting the information she just read.

The cat walks past again. It is a big tom-cat. You can see its big balls, when it starts to turn away from the glass. It is stripy and much bigger than a normal pet cat.

Rachel starts to giggle. I just nod silently. I don't really want to talk to her. She has been in an almost giddy mood ever since we entered the zoo. Sometimes skipping like a little girl in hope of some ice-cream. It does not suit her though. In her constant drunken state she keeps tripping and swaying. It is a borderline miracle she isn't constantly bumping into people. Or maybe not. Maybe it is in the nature of things. Though loud and clumsy, she navigates her way through this public space undetected. But there are only very few people around right now.

When the cat decides not to appear again from behind the rock, possibly to take a nap somewhere or hide for a bit from the inappropriate stares of all those visitors, I turn to see the next animal. Rachel has already run ahead just to shout back.

"Did you know, the foot-flagging frog does not croak as it lives in very noisy surroundings, such as near waterfalls. He would not be heard by other members of his species. Which is kind of crap if he wants to get jiggy with any of the lady frogs, I guess. Soooo – he has come up with a system to communicate by flagging his feet in all sorts of ways. Like those dudes at the airports with their flags. God, that is stupid! Hahahaha..." Rachel starts laughing hysterically and waves both her arms in the air like a mad woman. Of course this makes her lose her balance, so she stumbles and crashes into a litter bin.

I try to ignore the loud noise and her snorting giggle.

"OUCH – you silly whore... hahaha!"

The frogs are quite hard to find in their tank. Very small creatures. After a while I find three of them sitting very still on rocks and wet branches in-between leaves. Behind me there is a loud waterfall crashing into a small pond that seems to have the favourite rock of a huge and very lazy iguana.

There is no foot flagging going on in the tank.

The amphibians are very still. While Rachel noisily tries to get up again and fails several times, I stare at them. Nothing. Maybe they have nothing to say to each other anymore. All said and done. No more mating urge. Or they are too afraid to put themselves out there. If you keep your mouth shut or your feet still, you can't get hurt. Or maybe they are having some quiet time. Let's have a break and shut the fuck up for a little while. It will do us all some good, they might have flagged with their feet at some point in agreement. Or it is a remembrance moment for George, the frog, who is no longer with us anymore. Amen.

I close my eyes for a moment. There are no other visitors near-by. It is still relatively early in the morning. Most visitors, especially parents with their overly-excited or tired or tantrum-throwing or bored children will swamp the place in a little while. But right now it is still quiet.

I immediately see Martin's face again. Laughing. He had asked me what I did for a living. I felt daring. Confident. A little too excited. I could have told him anything. I knew, I would not see him again. Anything. I told him I was a writer. Proud of that manuscript in the car, I went for the truth. Well, a truth so close now to my grasp, that it felt like I was actually a writer. A finished manuscript.

And then – he laughed.

"Oh look, over here..." Rachel is back on her feet, running and shouting. "Pygmy hippos!"

With a little sigh, I open my eyes again. My face feels hot. It might be the heat of the huge tropical hall we are in, that tries to simulate the climate of rainforests across the globe. My hair is already damp not only from sweating, but from the humidity.

Rachel bangs her head against the glass to see the pygmy hippos walking under water.

"Cool!"

She starts to jump up and down. Then she turns around to throw up in the litter bin she crashed into just moments ago. All that wrenching is slightly covered up by the loud waterfall behind us.

Ben is leaning against the concrete wall shaped to look like natural rock. He has been very quiet all morning. He tried to take my hand a few times. But I crossed my arms across my chest and tucked my hands away in my armpits, pretending I hadn't noticed his attempt to make contact. I can't look him in the eye. I cannot be touched by him right now.

Rachel skips over to me. In a swinging motion she tries to wrap her arms around my waist and swing me around. Of course we both lose our balance and Rachel crashes on the ground, lands right in the middle of a puddle. Again, no-one is around, thank God, to see my stumbling moment.

"Shit", Rachel wipes her muddy hand on her skirt.

"Crap! My ass is soaking wet", she shrieks. "I look like I pissed and shat myself all at once!" She finds the thought hilarious and starts to laugh again.

I use the opportunity to walk past her.

"Hey! You are not even going to help me up, you selfish cow!"

Don't turn around. Don't talk. Don't engage. Let her be.

His laughter was not good-natured. He was laughing at me. At the idea, that I might have something to say. The idea, that I even thought, I might have something to say. Martin thought the notion of me writing was just too ludicrous. I might as well have told him, that I was a flower psychiatrist, a ghost whisperer, a painter waiting to get a job on the moon. A writer, don't be ridiculous. You?

We had been talking for a while. I thought, it went all very well. Even a little flirtatious. He seemed interested. I even thought a little smitten for a moment. I wanted to impress him. I told him about my proudest achievement. My creative baby in the car. The paper-stack underneath the passenger seat.

Oh how ridiculous.

"Okay... I will humour you", he then said rolling his eyes. "What schmalzy story did you cook up. I bet it is some corny love story. Right? Some fantasy about the knight in shining armour, that shags you till you are sore. Come on, love, tell me about your writing"

He said "writing" in such a mocking tone, that I was unable to speak. Though I know I should stand up for my baby. Defend it. Be there. Show my love for it. Stand by it. This is me. I should have shouted out loud. I should have...

I could feel the blood draining from my face for a small moment, only to shoot back up with ferocious vengeance, setting my cheeks on fire.

Some cabin neighbour started talking to Martin about the meat on the grill being well done. He seemed glad to have an excuse to leave me there.

Rachel and Ben were watching me from the dark sidelines. I have never seen Rachel so focussed, her eyes almost piercing, never blinking once, not moving a muscle. She seemed sober for the first time. Not needing a drink.

Ben looked agitated. As if in pain. He did not come to bed with me that night. I was almost relieved.

Rachel grabs me by the elbow and drags me further down the circular route through the artificial rainforest. I don't even try to resist. I let her push and shove me around. Almost listen to her announcements in front of every new habitat, always starting with "Did you know...?" Ben always a little behind us, never looking up.

The komodo dragon gets Rachel's attention more than any of the other animals. The deadly bite. The fact that the huge saurian does not kill his prey immediately, but infects them with a protein or poison that makes them bleed to death once bitten, seems to especially delight her. It even preys on its young. So the babies spend their first couple of years up trees and in large bushes to be safe from the vicious hunger of their parents. Until they are big enough to defend themselves or until they are just too fat and heavy to get onto the protective branches.

After leaving the cabins before dawn, I decided I needed a break from driving very early on. Ben had no distraction to offer in the car. No cheerful chatter. Just an absent look on his face. So when the road sign for the zoo came up, I did not even think twice. I did not anticipate though, that Rachel would be joining us from now on. I wanted to have a quiet walk. Pretend to concentrate on the animals. Ignore Ben. Give myself a little break. Watch chimpanzees throw faeces. Adore the small panda. Be in awe of the tiger. Admire some elephants and rhinos or even giraffes. Maybe have some coffee. Some cake or maybe some deep-fried food. But Rachel would not be ignored.

We walk around for hours. Rachel keeps talking, falling over, laughing, spitting, throwing up, stumbling, crashing into bins and trees. Her face has bumps and bloody cuts. But she keeps talking and skipping. Drunkenly glass-eyed with a slightly vicious twinkle.

I don't care anymore. Without giving it a second thought, I follow her around the zoo like a little puppy drained of all energy.

My baby is still in the car. Underneath that passenger seat. Waiting for me.

Unprotected.

ANNA

I am on the floor. My head is pounding. For a moment I can't remember how I got here. The wood is cool against my temple. I think I am bleeding as there is some liquid running down my forehead. They are screaming. I am used to Rachel screaming. But I have never heard Ben in such an uproar. I can't make out any words.

Just noise.

I must have fallen and hit my head on the edge of the desk again. That happens, when Rachel comes at me with disdain. When she runs up from behind and crashes into my chair. The laptop screen already has a little crack from one of our collisions.

I can hear Rachel laughing. That spitting laugh. And then there is a crashing sound. I force myself to lift my head. There is indeed blood on the floor. More than I thought. I push myself up onto my knees and then my wobbly legs, everything around me is swimming. I try to get some balance by holding on to my desk for a moment. Then I start climbing down the stairs. The shouts have come from the kitchen. It is silent right now. An eerie silence.

Ben is pacing. His eyes fixed on the same spot on the floor. I assume he is looking at Rachel, when she starts to laugh again.

"Is that all you've got? Are you already out of arguments, pretty boy? Really? You need to hit me to get your point across? Very convincing..."

I can hear her spitting.

"Shut up!"

I have never seen Ben this angry.

"You can't save her, pretty boy. Give it up. She belongs to me, pretty boy. Ugly, hopeless ickle little me! Ha!"

I hold on to the banister. They have not noticed me there.

He starts crying and falls onto one of the chairs next to the dining table which I never use.

"Whoops... that was easy."

Rachel gets up, wobbling over to Ben, who buries his face in his hands.

"You can't have her."

Ben is whispering now, so I can hardly hear him.

"You can't have her. She belongs with me. She is special. She will make it."

"So invested ... oooohh...", Rachel mockingly coos. Then she leans in and starts to whisper to him. Her voice changes. Seductively she starts to caress his hair.

"You know what happens, when you put your hopes in the wrong person, Benny. Don't you. Hearts get broken. Give up. Make it easy for us all. And I will end it. She will listen to me. You hear. She will listen to me. She is fragile enough to listen."

"No!"

Rachel lets go of him and laughs loudly again. Full of disdainful pity.

"Okay... Have it your way, Benny-Boy. I leave her to you... for a while. It is much more fun that way anyway. Watching you two fail. You embarrassing little pair. With your embarrassing little ambitions. Go ahead. What do I care? I have got time. I am not going anywhere anytime soon anyway."

I starting to feel woozy.

Rachel has gone.

"Ben?"

He immediately looks up and starts towards me.

I fall.

It's all turning to darkness.

SUNDAY

I can almost feel the bedsprings through the thinly worn material of the mattress. There is a shelf with books on it. There is a thick layer of undisturbed dust on all of them. I feel almost sorry for them. Left to be ignored till they fall apart. Captain Ahab forever chasing his big white whale. Lizzy trying to ignore the aloof Mr. Darcy, while falling deeply in love. Count Dracula draining Lucy Westenra, Max Brooks dreaming up a world overrun by zombies, Richard Dawkins speaking out against religion, some tattered cheap erotic novels, a penny dreadful and of course a copy of the bible and a road map.

The room smells mouldy. I am sure that the bathroom has not been carefully cleaned after the last one-night resident had a shower in there. So I will skip that part of staying in a motel. Even though tomorrow is the big day, I don't care, whether I smell right now or not. Maybe tomorrow morning. Maybe.

There are only very few miles left. We could have driven on into the city. One or two more hours. I don't know exactly. Looked for a nice hotel. Or even taken up residence in the room I have chosen for the next couple of weeks. A fine restaurant to celebrate. To prepare. Or order some food in. We could have. The idea of sitting down in an office so soon, working on the manuscript. It does not feel real anymore.

I had a long stop at a café in the afternoon. Somewhere next to the road. I tried to eat something. A sandwich or something. But nothing on the menu seemed to be right. It took forever to order a BLT-sandwich. The waitress got quite impatient with me after a while. I did not even pretend to be sorry. I got a cup of coffee as well. It was the worst coffee in a long while. Bitter and not exactly hot anymore. I did not complain. Ben did not say a word. I was grateful.

The café had a stack of old magazines. And a few new ones, I guess. To stop me from just staring out of the window, I picked up a few and flicked through them. I have no idea what stories they contained. Celebrities, I guess. Rising stardom. Falling stars. Weight gain and loss. Beauty advice, I guess. Some new royal baby somewhere. Scandals. Fashion, maybe. Maybe even something interesting. I would be very hard pushed to give any account of which magazines I had in my hands that afternoon. Two hours. That is much longer than I had intended. But I just could not bring myself to get up again. Ben did not seem to mind. He shut down. I forgot to tip the waitress appropriately, which earned me an annoyed eye-roll. I did not care enough to correct the mistake. She had to put up with me for two whole hours. Blocking the table from better-paying customers.

I unwrap a fatty burger I got in a drive-thru half an hour ago. It is still lukewarm. I have a few bites and then a sip from my water-bottle and leave the half eaten burger on the night-stand. I think I might not finish it after all. I have cramps and desperately need the toilet now.

I am glad I saw that program on television the other day. They said that the long lasting belief that you could get STDs from toilets was just fake news. The origin behind it was quite interesting. British doctors had cooked up this deception to get people to be less ashamed about sexually transmitted diseases and get examinations and consequently treatment. Sitting down on a contaminated toilet, that seemed less indecent than fucking with some disease-infested person, who is either not your spouse, or maybe even worse is your spouse, but shagging some other infected person behind your back. This is how syphilis is spread, right? Doctors knew better, but they told the toilet lie to give their patients the benefit of a hopeful doubt. All bullshit in the name of superficial propriety. Decent, decent.

I groan, while I am on the revoltingly dirty toilet. My insides are twisting and grumbling.

"Oh fuck…"

It takes a while before I am empty and my guts start to calm down.

After I roughly clean up the faecal Jackson Pollack I produced, and which just won't go away by merely flushing, I just want to crawl into bed. The smell of the now cold burger stirs my stomach unkindly again. So I force myself to first throw it in the trash, before I get under the blanket. For a second I think about all the people, who have slept in this room. All those sad stories, that led them here. The heart-break. The misery. I don't get to delve too much into that train of thought though, before I fall asleep.

ANNA

"And they lived happily ever after...", Ben looks at me and smiles.

I feel empty. It's done... More or less. A little filling up here and there. A short additional scene. A little editing. A closing scene maybe. The happy ending I have worked towards is here. No more obstacles. Right? I am glad I threw out everything and started again. Fresh. Completely different. I don't remember how many times I have started again. But this time, Ben thinks I got it right.

"It's nice", Ben walks over and gives me a reassuring smile. "Very sweet. You can be proud."

He is right. I never thought I would get this far. Never thought, I would go through with this. Have a proper love story. And the wedding was in spring. It was just lovely. Thank you very much. The end. Tip my hat, if I had one, to Jane Austen. The master. The Queen of Romance. Thank you so much, dearest teacher.

I feel like crying. I have heard about those cases. Writers feeling empty after finishing a story. They have to say goodbye to their creations. Say goodbye to their world. It feels strange to do. To give it up to a readership perhaps. A scary prospect. Letting go. Naturally. But this is different. I didn't realise until now. It slowly dawns on me, what I have to do.

"This isn't right. This is not it. I am not done yet", I look at Ben.

Pleading.

It takes a moment for him to understand. He shakes his head. "No, no, no... don't."

Now it is Ben, who is pleading.

"Leave it be. It's your first. Leave it. Let them be happy. There are loads of other stories you can write. In time. Loads more. Happy, tragic, funny, dark, horrible, thrilling... anything. Leave it. Happy ending. Nice, right? Romance. Boy meets girl. Greatest story ever told. Remember?"

"I am not done. This is not it..." It sounds like an apology. But I don't really feel sorry. There is nothing to be sorry about. It just is what it is. Inevitably. Free will of the writer, my ass!

"Come on, it is fiction. You have the power over it. It is your story. You can have it any way you want it. You can be done, whenever you want it to be done. Let it end on a happy note."

I turn away from Ben and face my laptop. For a split second I think I can see Rachel's sneering reflection in the window. Hear her laugh. But I must have imagined it.

Ben is still talking, but I can't hear what he is saying anymore. I put my hands back on the keys. I have no choice in this. My story. My creation. Do I drive my story, or does my story drive me? I have no idea. I am just certain, that I am not finished. This is not, where Emma and Adam are going to end up. I am not sure though what story I want to tell instead. Or what is still missing. I just feel the pull towards the keyboard. The need to carry on. Not to let go yet.

MONDAY

The morning sun feels warm against my skin. A slight breeze. The smell of grass. Leaves. Insects humming. A few birds.

I left the car at a gravelly space next to the road. Not exactly a car park, but it had to do. I have four hours left before I have to meet the editor. There is only about half an hour's drive left till the edge of the city. Maybe a little less. So I have some time left on my hands. Time maybe to go and get something to eat. A coffee. A decent one for once. Foamy maybe. Maybe.

Time.

I needed a walk. So I just stopped.

Ben and Rachel are nowhere to be found. I haven't seen Rachel since our trip to the zoo.

Skipping, happy, vomiting Rachel.

Even though I tried to ignore her, I almost started to like this side of her.

I think I saw Ben yesterday in the shabby armchair next to the bookshelf in the motel. But maybe I was imagining things. I am so used to seeing Ben in armchairs. I'm not sure he was there last night.

The grass is still a little damp. My feet are cold. I try to wrap myself a little tighter in the woolly cardigan. It is too thin though. I keep walking. Next to the field is a wood. Some conifers I am not able to identify. The path is broken up by thick tyre marks. A tractor perhaps. Some heavy machinery. I just keep walking for a while. The path leads up a bit of a hill. When I reach its top, I am slightly out of breath. I have been neglecting my walks in the past couple of weeks. It shows.

Ever since I abandoned Emma, sent her and Adam into the void, I have been writing non-stop.

My baby.

It would have never had a chance with Emma and Adam still around.

There is a big rock. I sit down, it is surprisingly warm. There are no trees on the other side of the path. Just a field. So the sun had no obstacles to stop it from warming up the rock.

I close my eyes and try to breathe. Calm down. My heart is racing. Sweat is covering my face and I can feel it on my back, under my breasts and on the inside of my thighs.

Breathe.

Calm. Calm.

When I open my eyes again, I get black spots from the brightness of the sun and it takes a while to adjust to the light.

I suddenly spot something in the grass in front of me. I blink to get my vision back on track. It takes me a while to realise that it is a dead fox. Its body looks half squashed. Tyre tracks. It must have been ill or already injured. I can't imagine a fox being caught by surprise by a loud heavy tractor, roaring on its way along the field. The fox was already broken. It must have been. It does not make any sense otherwise. This was the final straw. Perhaps a welcome end. Or maybe it was already dead, when it was crushed even more. Bones broken. Organs mangled to a bloody mess.

Mangled.

It must have died a few days ago. The small animals of the forest have already started gorging on its body. Maggots, ants, flies... they are all invited to the party and have accepted the invitation aplenty. One of its eyes is already missing. Its are lips pulled back, exposing the teeth in a grotesque grin.

I can't take my eyes off the animal. I can see him degenerate tiny bit by bit. Shrinking to furry leftovers.

I am unable to move.

The sun is almost down. Creating a beautifully rich and

warm yellow light. Stretching the shadows of the trees next to the road. I am the only one on the road. The light is calming.

There have been a few missed calls on my mobile phone. All from the editor. A few messages left, too. I do not listen to them. I know what they are about. The phone must have been ringing all day. I feel a little sorry for her and her ruined day. Well, not ruined day. But messed up schedule for the day. But it can't be helped.

The avenue looks beautiful. Large trees. Apple trees. All lined up next to the road. A mile long maybe. Maybe less. I don't know. They just fly by. All those apple trees. Sturdy branches. Thick trunks. I did not know that apple trees could grow that tall. They must have been planted a long time ago. Apple trees are usually not the tree of choice, when it comes to avenues. I would guess picking those apples next to the road with cars flying by is not exactly anyone's idea of a health-oriented orchard. Maybe it was a mistake. A wrong order. Orchestrated in some city hall. Some small-time clerk making a mistake. It would have been too expensive to correct the mistake. Maybe this used to be an orchard and they just desperately needed this road, leaving just two lines of trees for decoration. Who knows.

All those inviting apple trees. So sturdy. So sturdy. Flying by. Inviting me.

I can hear Rachel's cackling laugh. It sounds almost gentle. Almost.

"Come to me... Come... don't be afraid...It is so easy... Come..."
Flying by. Flying by.
"Come..."

EMMA

The wind was not that strong, but a little icy. Emma could feel the cold surface of the park bench through her long woolly coat. Usually she would not have sat down in the middle of the park. She would have gone home or looked for a café perhaps. Somewhere comfortable. But all of that did not matter right now.

The doctor had had that serious tone of voice. The one they put on, when they have bad news. Emma didn't remember what she had to say. The crass difference in the tone of voice stopped her brain from functioning in a normal way. She had been so giddy the last time. Shown her all the little details. Printed out a picture. Been almost sickeningly sweet. Emma had felt it was inappropriate to talk like that in her capacity as a doctor. Now she wished she would do it again.

But the playful voice was gone.

All Emma could hear was 'no heartbeat'. Nothing else was able to make it through to her. The limbs, the back, the belly, the face in profile, even all the little fingers... it was all still there. The same ultrasound like last time. But no pumping behind the little ribcage.

"I am so sorry", the doctor said, never breaking eye contact.

Emma took out the picture from the ultrasound she had been carrying around with her. She was sure it was a girl. The doctor had not committed to a clear statement regarding the sex, but had hinted at it. A daughter. Her daughter.

No heartbeat.

The little munchkin suddenly became the foetus. The object that needed removing. How cruel a shift in register can be. Loving terms, replaced by medical phrasing.

No heartbeat.

The happiness turned into talk about a procedure. The possible risks. The likelihood of a damaged reproductive system. Barren. What an antiquated term.

No heartbeat.

Emma put her hands around her slightly swollen belly. The remains of her short motherhood. All those possibilities. Taken away in an instant.

No heartbeat.

And that was that.

Adam did not know yet.

Emma knew that she would not be able to be with him anymore. She could not explain it. But she knew. All those happy months in love. They did not matter anymore. They became irrelevant so quickly. Just one instance. All the laughs. The giggling. The passion. The love-making. All those kisses. His sweet breath. Their incredible conversations. All that happiness. All gone. Washed away. From now on, it was just her and her lost daughter. There was no room for daddy. Her dead daughter would not be ripped from his body, but hers. This was hers. Only hers. He had no place in her loss. He would have to deal with his heartbreak on his own. Emma felt sorry for Adam for a moment. It was not his fault. None of it was. She would abandon him in his pain. But he was already too removed from her heart for it to truly matter.

It also didn't matter anymore, that she had had her doubts about the pregnancy. Her motherhood. Would she manage to be there for her child? Those questions had tortured her for the past couple of weeks. How could anyone be there for someone else so unconditionally? Love them. No matter what. Emma was sure, that this wasn't her. Her belly, growing bigger week by week, felt like a cage, blowing up to trap her inside. Lose herself. It didn't matter anymore. The guilt. The absence of happiness. How could she admit that to anyone. Even Lilly. Or even herself for that matter.

Just hormones. Just hormones.

The new mantra supposed to make it all okay. Turn her into a mother eventually. Nature taking care of the nurture. None of Adam's joyous escapades at the news, could bring her reassurance that everything would be fine. The cage of motherhood was looming threateningly over her morning sickness, that seemed to have the smell of burnt frozen fish fingers.

In death, she was suddenly able to embrace her daughter. Once the relief, the shame, the guilt had washed away.

"Just you and me, little one."

No heartbeat. No heartbeat. No heartbeat.

The wind got stronger.

"Just you and me."

ANNA

"Why?"

Ben looks upset.

"This has nothing to do with what you were building up to. Why?"

"Mothers...and daughters..." I am whispering. I am not sure, what I am saying. I look at him not sure how to explain something I am hardly able to grasp myself. I look at the page. This last chapter. My goodbye to Emma. I am sending her off into my creative void. A broken women. No more hope. I am a cruel woman. Oh for shame.

Shame, shame, shame.

"I am done..."

I close the laptop.

"Done..."

I get up and walk down the stairs. I don't look at Ben. I can't. He is heartbroken. At least for now. I hope he will be able to forgive me soon. For I will need him. Very soon. Because then we will start again. The demon is exorcised. The ever lurking demon of motherhood. The insecurities. Everything too close. Too close. We will start all over again. Not today though. We find our story. Not the greatest story ever told. I am not Jane Austen. That is abundantly clear.

But my story.

My own.

The one for a possible public. I know it. I have shat out my other story. The one I had to get out. Kitschy. Heart broken. Insecure. Not all of it. Sure. There is enough left that, I am not ready to face yet. I have barely scratched the surface. But enough to make room. Clear my tortured and twisted being to let in a story. A story to make Ben proud. My muse. To make him smile. To be happy with me. To defeat Rachel. Laugh in her face for a change. Not with disdain. But with relief. Grateful.

I needed to shit it out. All the drivel. Make room. Make room. For here I come.

I feel free. Liberated. I suddenly feel like the writer I want to become. The one, who finds her story. Not just start over again and again to find some kind of structure that will do. But find the story. The one that matters. The one I am meant to write. Only me. There is room now. I am hungry. All those wonderful possibilities. All those stories that need to have nothing to do with me and my demons. I am confident that it is right there now. Close enough to reach. I feel the pull of all the right words out there.

I put on some coffee. No ritual. No foam. Just coffee and milk in a big mug.

The garden looks nice. It has some structure to it now. The leaves are turning yellow already. I will have to ask Lucas to help me put the leaves into a big pile. Prepare for winter. I will need those gloomy days to write. To write my novel. My story. I will miss our talks on the terrace. The adventures. The explorers. All those wonderfully strange worlds beneath volcanos or in the middle of yet untouched wilderness, rainforest. Weapon making technology from the stone age. Or the knights of the round table.

He is not afraid of me anymore. I am sure of it. He has become quite a chatter box. Maybe it is the sweets I offer him. He has almost reached his goal for the telescope. I hope, he will pick a new goal next year. I will miss him otherwise. There is nothing to do in the garden in winter. Our garden work has become a weekly ritual over the course of the summer. It will give me time to write.

Till next spring. If he is still willing.

The last apples need picking. I might make some apple juice

tonight. Or make jelly. I haven't decided yet. I might have to go to the shops to buy some sugar though. I want to get some biscuits for Lucas as well. And go to the book store. I am sure he hasn't read Jules Verne's adventures of Captain Nemo yet. It is right up his alley. A must-have.

The birds in the apple tree seem to be having an energetic brawl.

I am done. For now. For a brief moment. For a little breather. For a tiny break.

I am happy, I guess.

I can hear her laughing. Spitting.

I ignore her and watch the birds in the apple tree.

I am hopeful. I know my great story now. And I will write it. With Ben.

EPITAPH

My mother was never one of the motherly kinds. She was never around. To be precise, she left when I was three. I am not sure how available she was before her departure. Her disappearing act. Her turning her back on us. Or whatever you want to call her decision. Abandonment.

I remember only little of the time before. I remember her mostly from a distance. Her in the kitchen, while I was watching her from the corridor. Her sitting on the porch, while I was playing in the sandbox in the garden. But I also remember sitting on her lap. Her reading stories. A few absent-minded kisses on the forehead. Her lovely smell. I remember a lullaby. Not the exact words. The melody always just a little beyond my reach. Slipping away every time I seem to remember enough to attempt humming it.

I hated her for a while. It helps and I can highly recommend it. Hate a little for a while. Get it out of your system. It took me way too long to get to that point of hate. I did not hang around there for long though. It is not really recommended to wallow in hate either. Get it over with quickly.

I blamed myself of course. I must have been a horrible child. Too stressful to hang on to. Too boring perhaps. Too stupid. Too ugly. Too insignificant. Not lovable enough to capture my mother's heart. Maybe. Maybe. I had every explanation in the world ready to belittle myself and take the blame. It's nothing unusual. Children do this. They so willingly take on the whole weight of the world to explain their parents' bad behaviour.

When I got older I worked hard to dismiss the blame. I

reasoned that I was far too little to have any blame in the unfortunate events of my childhood. I was not to blame. Impossible. People break up. Marriages fail. Some women feel trapped. She must have been very unhappy to have left her baby behind. She had to sacrifice the love of her life to save herself. It was perhaps a brave act of female liberation. I was suddenly convinced that she must have loved me dearly. She must think of me every day. Miss me. Wonder about me. My life, my future. I was determined to make her proud. I was determined to give her a reason to come back one day, meet me and smile with overflowing pride.

"Look at you, honey. Look at what you have become. So proud. So proud."

I worked hard. When she didn't turn up, I worked even harder. Make mummy proud.

Apparently it was never good enough. Not good enough to get her attention. To convince her it was worth coming back for me. Her wonderfully accomplished daughter. I did not realise that she never found out about all of my hard work. How could she?

When she didn't come, the old mechanism of self-blame kept kicking back in. I was not good enough. I was not beautiful enough. Not clever enough. My grades in school were not good enough. My university degree was not good enough. My handsome boyfriend was not good enough. My lovely well-kept flat was not good enough.

The little red-bricked chapel at the edge of the graveyard looks peaceful in the middle of all the trees and the bushes. I can understand, why she wished to be buried here. This graveyard surrounded by a little wood. Birds singing. Enough shade to keep you cool even during the heat-waves of July and August. Enough trees to keep out the stormy nights in the autumn. Enough space to let in the rays of sunshine in spring to wake up the flowers.

I hate my black dress. It feels so false. So much like putting on a show. A costume for the occasion. I refused to wear a veil. A black ribbon would have to do to keep my hair in check. My grandmother is angry with me. She tried to insist on a veil. She even bought one for me. Pushed it in my face. It's a bittersweet day for her. Her daughter-in-law is gone for good. The woman that ruined everything. The one she loved to hate. All those hateful tirades, my father would at first try to hush and then just accepted, he had to endure every once in a while. Now she was gone, and grandma had to find a new favourite person to hate. You don't talk ill of the dead. That is something my grandma used to say all the time. There is a time for gossip. But once someone kicks the bucket, it was time to stop all ill-talk in grandma's house. It was one of her righteous rules, she stuck to. You could only escape her venomous tongue by escaping life. When the undertaker contacted us, I could almost hear her grind her teeth and bite her tongue. I am sure she regretted her rule that day. She had got so used to her tirades.

The bells are slightly out of tune. It sounds quite charming, once you get used to it.

The windows of my car start to mist over a little. The chapel's red bricks turn to a washed out grey colour. Even though the rain stopped a while ago, there are still constant drops of water dripping from the trees.

I am still not sure I want to get out of the car and make my way to the chapel, when a loud bang on the window makes me jump.

"Come on, sweetie. The service starts in five minutes."

My grandmother is determined to be punctual. My mother has been unreliable all her life, she said. At least now, let's do this right. As if being punctual has anything to do with reliability. Or with what happened with my mother. Or rather, what did not happen. Because nothing ever did happen. Once she had left. That was it. Nothing. Not a peep. Not a letter. No phone-call. She might as well have been dead for all I knew. The issue wasn't a few moments of waiting past an arranged time of the day. But I guess, that is grandma's way of shoving it to my mum without speaking ill of the dead.

Her bang on my window sets me in motion. The time to

contemplate whether or not to go to the funeral is over. I am going. Grandma's bang has taken the option of fleeing the scene from me. The good girl is going to her mother's funeral. End of discussion.

I started to make excuses for her. Dreamed up scenarios of why she had to leave. Falling in love, when I was most kind. Falling in with the wrong crowd, when I was pessimistic. A spy, who had to protect her beloved family, when I was most fanciful. But no matter how my stories to protect her good name came about, I was always certain that those dreamt up reasons were not part of the truth.

Reaching adulthood, I got a sense that it might have been a little more complicated than that. She might have felt trapped in her role as wife and mother. All those expectations from society of how to be. It might have been too much. Maybe she needed to break free of those chains. That cage. Maybe it was suffocating her. She could not take me with her on her journey of freedom. No matter what she felt about me or how I might have behaved. It might not have had anything to do with me.

Maybe she just never found her place in motherhood. Being a mother is scary. It is not just cuddles with a chubby little cutie-pie. It is not just changing nappies and pushing a pram. Motherhood can be daunting. Not every woman finds her fulfilment there. Nature does not always kick in, the way it is supposed to. I have seen it in friends. Most stick it out. A sense of duty and inevitability. Maybe my mother couldn't. Maybe it was a good thing to have an absent mother rather than a miserable failed one. Maybe her hormones just did not do their job. Who knows, what happened? Who knows, what she felt? What her motivation was? It has taken me a lot of time and energy to bring myself to believe that I did not drive her away with a snotty nose, unreasonable tantrums and an overall unlovable disposition. Still, I am not always completely convinced.

There are about a dozen people already seated. The music is light and impersonal. The pastor makes uncommitted conversation with everyone walking through the door. As soon as he gets hold of my father and grandmother, I squeeze past them to take my seat on the far left. I am really not in mood for small-talk. A simple casket covered with a few flowers, nothing expensive, and a framed picture that looks like one you put on a job application. Apparently she had worked for a local newspaper and this was the picture they used to accompany the few articles that require a picture of the author. At least that is what my dad told me. The pastor had called him, once he had found out, we were family, to get a better picture. But of course we did not have any picture from this decade.

On the right side of the chapel in the second row is a young boy, maybe twelve or thirteen years old. His eyes are red from crying. He looks horribly upset. His mother keeps putting her arm around his shoulders and pulls him close to comfort him. It seems, he is the only one in the room who has been crying. The only one, who cares.

There is a group of women, who don't seem to give a shit about my grandmother's rule. Gossip is so much fun. When they take their seats behind me, I try to shut out their conversation. But in vain. They pretend to whisper, but make sure it is loud enough for every one in the group to hear every word.

"I am really surprised, anyone came at all. I honestly thought, we would be the only ones to turn up."

"I know. I would have stayed at home, if I had know. But it is too sad, if no-one turns up for your funeral."

"Well, what did she expect. You can't be such a grumpy tight-lipped cow all your life and then expect a big turn-out."

They started to giggle.

"Oh – shoosh – you are so awful... haha...". Loud clearing of throats.

One woman – with particularly loud lipstick and thick blue eye-shadow – taps me on the shoulder.

"So sorry for you loss", she says with clearly pretend concern.

I sigh and then turn around.

"Thank you."

I really want to leave it at that and turn back to face forward. But she just won't let it go. She taps me on the shoulder again.

"So... how did you know the deceased?"

I struggle for a moment as I really don't want to talk to her. But what is the use. So I turn back and try to smile politely. I will never see her again after today anyway. So I opt for honesty.

"Anna Bennik was my mother", I say, struggling more than I thought I would.

I did not expect to see such shock in their eyes.

"Oh... her daughter?... Oh... I thought... you... we all thought... ehm... nevermind... ehm... sorry for your loss. We used to work with her at the paper. She was a good journalist. Sorry for your loss." It shuts them up for a bit and I am grateful.

My father sits down next to me, joined by grandma. This seems to confuse the women behind us even more. But it shuts them all up long enough for a hasty service to proceed. No-one volunteered to say something special. No extra music. No speeches. Just a quick service. Then off to the grave we go.

As we walk behind the coffin, I can hear whispers going through the group of people. Not just the women from the paper. Everyone seems to be in a bit of excitement. Gossip spreading like wildfire. They are all walking behind us. The three of us are the only family that turned up, apparently. So the pastor thought it was only appropriate for us to lead the suppressed but excited whispers of the chattering pack.

"That is her daughter! And her husband!"

"Are you sure? I thought they were dead..."

"I know. Car accident."

"That was what she said."

"I always thought it was odd."

"No you didn't. You loved that gruesome story. The truck smashing into them."

"Don't be horrible."

"Maybe it is a different daughter..."

"You are so dense. Don't you see. She made up that story."

"She lied?"

"Of course she did. I always thought, she was a horrible woman. To disown your child like that. Oh what a horrible woman. No wonder, she ended up that way. Poetic justice, if you ask me. Killing them off, just like that."

My mind feels very numb. I hope that neither my grandmother nor my father are listening to the talk behind us. Otherwise they might forget about that stupid rule very quickly.

All those years, no matter what fanciful or pitiful scenario, what far-fetched or realistic sounding explanation I came up with on my mother disappearing from our lives, I always imagined her thinking of us. Remembering the good times. Maybe grieving on giving us up. Missing us. Or in my worst lowest self-worth moments thinking about all the reasons she had to kick us out of her now wonderful life.

But she killed us off. Gave us a horrible death in a car. We were gone. Not to be dealt with again. That would explain the silence. The lack of letters or phone-calls. You don't write to dead people. You don't call them.

My head is spinning. They all know. All those horrible chattering people behind us. Sneering. Enjoying the delightful scandal. The human misery. Oh how exquisite. They look like they can't wait to spread the news at the bakery or on the street, to their neighbour or friend on the phone.

I can already see the hole in the ground from afar.

Why?

All my explanations. Everything. Nothing makes sense anymore. She can't have hated us that much, as to feel the need to get rid of us so completely.

My father is walking beside me. I expect him to be grieving. To be uncomfortable. To be angry. To feel embarrassed by all the gossip, which he must have registered by now. To my surprise, he is none of these things. He seems liberated. He takes my hand, squeezes it lightly and gives me a smile.

And then it hits me. We can stop wondering. We can stop hoping. It is done. It is over. We can finally let her go. She is gone. For good. She had always been a strange presence in our lives. Through my grandma's tirades. My father's loving stories about their time together. Every story about my early childhood featured her. His feeble attempt to give me a mother. At least through remembered stories. Little anecdotes. Never any blame or attempt to explain. Just stories.

"Oh, your mother was such a crappy cook", he would suddenly remember laughing. "It is quite an art form to burn fish fingers to a crisp and still have them frozen on the inside." He would get the giggles, whenever he shared one of their cooking stories, which felt so familiar not just from listening to them over and over again. My father never judged. He left that to grandma. It was his job to keep the fond memories alive. Without any poison of betrayal or abandonment.

"She might have left me. But she gave me the greatest gift of all", he once said, when I asked about her leaving us. "You. And how can I not be thankful for that? Who gives a shit, whether she is here to share the experience? The important thing is, that we are here to live through it together. Let grandma talk. That is her way of dealing with it. A mother never likes it, when she sees her child scorned or hurt."

That gave fuel to the theory, that my mother just could not bear the idea of having to witness any harm or hurt that could and would ever hit me.

The men start to lower the coffin into the grave. The pastor mumbles a few last words. The little crowd tries to keep some respectful silence. Then everybody looks at us. The pastor takes a little shovel and throws some dirt into the grave. My father steps forward and does the same thing. Then grandma. When it is my turn, I feel tears welling up. My throat tightens and my knees feel like they belong to another person. Everyone around us seems to disappear. It is just me and my mother. In death, I am able to embrace my mother. Shovel in hand, time slows down.

I miss her. The little memory of her laughing at the mess in the kitchen washes over me. Her picking me up and putting a kiss on my dirty hands smeared with over-ripe banana bits. Her screeching and giggling at being sprayed with water while I am jumping up and down in the bathtub.

The tears are running in streams down my cheeks now. I throw the dirt into that graceless impersonal hole in the ground.

"Goodbye, mummy."

I almost choke as I whisper those words.

"Hold on!"

A man in a grey tweed jacket comes running after me, as I unlock the door of my car. I wanted to leave as quickly as possible. But it is very clear, that he is determined to talk to me.

"Yes?"

"Excuse me... Tessa?"

I nod. That is all I can do right now.

He looks at me in a very strange way. Not in that curious scandalised way the women did.

"I think I have something, that you should have."

He has a leather carrier bag with him and pulls out a package wrapped up in brown paper, tied together with some string.

"Your mother wrote this", he says. "It was with her in the car, when..."

He hands me the package. It is heavy. Instead of just thanking him and leaving, I unwrap it immediately. It is a neatly tied up stack of paper. A manuscript.

As I try to put the brown wrapping paper on the roof of my car to take a closer look at my mother's writing a few loose papers fall out of the stack. As I bend down to pick it up, my heart tightens. Three pictures are lying on the ground of the parking lot. Three pictures. A unicorn with a rainbow on the horn and the mane. A house with a family, mother, father and a little girl, holding hands. Flowers on the meadow and a sun in the corner. The third one is showing a car crash. The broken car and a tree. A tree full of big red apples. All three pictures are marked with my mother's handwriting. Tessa, age three.

When I look up, the man looks at me. His eyes so knowing. So compassionate.

"She could not bear having left you. She needed to erase you from her life. Get rid of all the evidence, that her beautiful daughter is out there, and she is missing every moment of it. The thought was unbearable. Get rid of all the guilt she could not face, to be able to keep on living. It was easier to grieve and then push the grief aside. She did not succeed in the end."

I am crying shamelessly now.

"I hope to see you again soon, Tessa", he says. Then he turns and walks away.

He does not have to tell me his name. I already know. It is Ben.

ACKNOWLEDGE-MENTS

A couple of years ago I read the autobiography by the English comedian Lee Mack, *Mack – The Life*. He recalls how he always wanted to be a comedian, but deemed this goal unreachable, as comedians were special people. He did not see himself as special. He became a comedian anyway and to his surprise found out, that those he had admired were not that special after all. The difference being, they took the leap and just did it.

Ever since I can remember, I wanted to be a writer. A novelist even. But that seemed unreachable. Writers, especially novelists, were special people. I never saw myself as special. For a long time I chose to find the written word by studying literature and working as a journalist. Then I read Lee Mack's simple realisation. And though it seemed obvious, something clicked in knowing someone else had felt that way. I was finally ready to take the leap.

I told my husband about my wish to write. He immediately bought me a used laptop on Ebay and every now and then took our kids to the park, playground or zoo and send me to a Starbucks café for a few hours to put my fingers on those keys and start typing. Being a full-time mum of three most and foremost for the next couple of years, it took quite a while before a story started to form and my goal to call myself a writer, even a novelist, finally started to look reachable. All because, Lee Mack's realisation pushed down that barrier, that held me back for so many years.

Therefore, I want to start thanking people by thanking Lee Mack first.

I would also like to thank my friend Andrea Schartner, a former colleague and also mother of three, who inspired me infinitely by taking the leap first around that time, putting her stories to paper and self-publishing her beautiful novels via Amazon. She was the first to listen to my first outlines, which I hesitantly shared. To my surprise, she took them seriously, added some vital ideas that significantly shaped the structure of this book and read the first draft, despite it being in English. More thanks go to the wonderful author and friend Petra Hartmann, who kept encouraging me for years to write and who was one of the first to read the book and give really helpful feedback. My professor and friend Hans-Werner Breunig for commenting in real time via WhatsApp his reading experience and offering his literary expertise by filling the manuscript with comments and corrections. Thank you sooo much to Kate Sturrock, who proof-read the English original, and my Dad, who did the same with the German version, that followed. Even though he had expected something quite different, a lot more straightforward and less complicated to come from his daughter. It took him a while to warm up to the story, coming to the conclusion that you have to read it twice to appreciate it. Most people probably won't make the effort though. Thank you to my mother for reading the book while it was still in its English version, constantly apologising, that her lack of knowledge of the English language did not allow her to proceed any faster. My stepmother Beate for always telling me, that she thought I was talented and that she could not wait to read what stories I would find. My best friend Silke for reading the story and immediately pushing it onto her always reading family. My friend Daphne for proof-reading some late additional text. And of course my children, who so naturally refer to Mum as a writer, as if this is a given, and not something you might deem unreachable at all, always coming up with wonderful stories they want to write with me.

But most of all I want to thank my husband for buying that old laptop – and updating it to a new one a few years into the process – , as well as pushing me out the door and sending me to that Starbucks at Leipzig's Augustusplatz. I guess, he was mostly driven by the hope the writing thing would eventually make us rich. Allowing him to retire and spend the rest of his life lazing around in the hammock in the garden or sawing some wood in the garage for some wonderful new project. Nevertheless, at the end of the day, he might just be happy with me finally proudly calling myself a writer.

Thank you all!

* 9 7 9 8 5 9 9 3 3 6 5 8 7 *